POTATO TREE

POTATO TREE

BY JAMES SALLIS

HOST PUBLICATIONS
AUSTIN, TX

Host Publications, Inc. 1000 East 7ᵗʰ, Suite 201, Austin, TX 78702

Layout and Design: Joe Bratcher & Anand Ramaswamy
Cover Art: Jakub Kalousek
Cover Design: Anand Ramaswamy

Library of Congress Catalog Number: 2006934723

ISBN: 978-0-924047-39-8 (hardcover)
ISBN: 978-0-924047-40-4 (softcover)

First Edition

TABLE OF CONTENTS

INTRODUCTION

I glance up from my work with considerable surprise to find that I've been at this for forty years now, and peering back across that gulf, at these stories that proved in many ways my bridge across, is exceedingly a strange experience. The slats in the suspension bridge range from my earliest published examples to quite recent ones, this collection comprising a retread of Host's earlier (and now out of print) *Limits of the Sensible World* along with the bulk of previously uncollected stories.

There have been four other collections, including my very first book, *A Few Last Words*, and *Time's Hammers*, an embryonic Collected Stories from the UK; there's even an omnibus volume, *A James Sallis Reader*, containing stories, poems, essays, and two novels. The Reader was a landmark for me, one of those things for which a writer in his heart of hearts longs – like those gorgeous uniform paperback editions of my Lew Griffin novels put out by Walker, or a novel going back almost immediately for a second print run, as *Drive* did.

Or like the *L.A. Times Book Review* running a cover feature on my work.

On the morning I began writing this introduction, I learned that I'm to be given a lifetime achievement award at next year's Bouchercon in Anchorage. Following my comment "Are you sure you have the right person?" and a quick trip to my doctor to see if maybe the Bouchercon folk know something I don't – oh, and emailing everyone I've met in the last forty years (I'm cool, but not *that* cool) – I got back to work reading proof for this collection.

A lifetime, huh? And this is where it all began.

Short stories are what I always wanted to write; I'm a novelist by default. Something about the transparency of the short story, its apparent lightness, took me in quite early on. While others relished sinking into novels, the rapture of those deeps, I loved most the sudden resurfacing from a story, holding my breath a moment longer and opening my eyes slowly to see if the world looked different.

And what do I see now, looking back at these stories, these strange mirrors?

Well, he was certainly brash enough, the young man who wrote those first stories. Had no idea what he was doing, of course, but he covered well. And squinting, I can just make out in the distance certain familiar figures. The courting of genre conventions and archetypes. A stress on civility as the cornerstone of civilization. The terror that comes when one feels existence shift beneath one's feet. Above all, perhaps, a tacit refusal to accept the scrim of reality, an absolute surety that other worlds exist behind, beside and in the exact same place as this one.

"Just a little bit of an interpretative dysfunction," the physician says in the title story here. "You just won't ever know if things are as they seem to you; they could be *quite* different."

Exactly.

A standing joke among fellow writers is that my mother must have been frightened by plots, since I so sedulously abjure them. From the evidence of these stories, such was the case early on, in a story like "Kazoo" (which is, in fact, my first published story), and later on, in those like "Moments of Personal Adventure" and "The Western Campaign." Storyline is always limned, always there–lurking about the wings like an understudy hoping to get onstage–but rarely drawn to the surface. There is, after all, so much *else* of interest. Getting the physical world down and true, gradations of complex emotions, suspensions of complex thought. Language itself. Or character: the many ways in which the world shapes us, the many ways in which we shape the perceived world to our own image.

So not a lot has changed from that first story in New Worlds to later ones in transatlantic review or Album Zutique.

I still don't know what I'm doing. And I *am* far less clever about it. But just as stubborn.

"Body in the floor," I tell interviewers and students who ask how I've persisted all these years at writing, working for the most part outside commercial conventions, following no sails but my own.

I go on: There's a body in the floor, and for a long time no one admits it's there, they just go on stepping over it and going about their business. But the body's still there. Then one day someone trips over it. "Look, there's a body in the floor." "My God!" "How long has *that* been there?"

Thanks for noticing.

I'll get up now.

— James Sallis
Phoenix, August 2006

ACKNOWLEDGMENTS

The Creation of Bennie Good copyright 1969, first appeared in *Orbit*, ed. Damon Knight.

How's Death? copyright 1995, first appeared in *Oasis*.

An Ascent of the Moon copyright 1990, first appeared in *South Dakota Review*.

I Saw Robert Johnson copyright 1989, first appeared in Ellery Queen's Mystery Magazine.

Men's Club appears here for the first time.

Others copyright 1985, first appeared in The Georgia Review.

Jane Crying copyright 1970, first appeared in the author's collection A Few Last Words.

Allowing the Lion copyright 1986, first appeared in *Florida Review*.

Only the Words Are Different copyright 1969, first appeared in *Orbit*, ed. Damon Knight.

Syphilis: A Synopsis copyright 2000, first appeared in *Quarter After Eight*.

Récits copyright 1970, first appeared in *transatlantic review*.

My Friend Zarathustra copyright 1970, first appeared in *Orbit*, ed. Damon Knight.

Free Time copyright 2003, first appeared in *Album Zutique*, ed. Jeff Vandermeer.

Bleak Bay copyright 2000, first appeared on *The Pedestal Magazine* website.

Alaska copyright 1994, first appeared in *Confrontation*.

Kazoo copyright 1967, first appeared in *New Worlds*.

To Dave and Pat

The Creation
Of Bennie Good

"Do you like my foot," putting it on the table. There, between the chipped saucer and candle; you have noticed how carefully I avoid the marmalade, the box of salty butter. "Will you accept it as a token of my affection? For you? It is, as they say, a good foot." Earlier, I have deftly undone the laces with my toes, grasped the sock between piano-key toes and foot and slowly drawn it off, like peeling a willow wand. "The arch is long and graceful, with the springy delicacy of a light man. The toes curl in as though to embrace the foot; the nails are flecked with color. And pink is the color of this foot." Pink, with the bright red crescent at the top of the curve: pimple on one side, in the curve, and dimpled on the other. "I am offering this, should you want it, my dear. It is all I have."

Her attention is arrested by my foot. This is true of most. At parties my friends will group together talking, and glancing occasionally with great expectation towards the corner chair where I sit calm, unmoved, unmoving. As the evening advances, their glances are more frequent and begin to form a rhythm; then finally, beginning as a low moan among the women, gradually swelling up through the groups until it becomes a steady, hard, syncopated shout, and bursting at last out of the crowd, the call comes: *Foot! Foot!* Then slowly I lift it to the level of their eyes and one of them, a woman, the chosen, comes forward out of the group wearing shyness like a belt and starts softly to undo the pale pink shoe, dropping it to the floor, where it lies on its side in the carpet pile. You have seen the way a snake is skinned – first the skin is slit away from the mouth, then rolled gently down along the body: this is how my sock is removed – then thrown to them. A few are unable to stand the pressure and must be sent away. Others on the edge near me remove their own shoes and socks and sit staring sadly at the pale uncovered feet. I tell her all this.

"It's all I have, it's yours." But this one, this Sally, is more moved than the rest. Already the tight black circles around her eyes are smearing, becoming less distinct; eyelids covered in green sequins are flashing like tiny chandeliers. Her little hands are perched on the rim of the cup and soon one will creep out across the ceramic dishes to shyly, lightly touch my foot. She is overwhelmed at the size of the occasion, the depth of my offer.

Perhaps I will make conversation; I've found this sometimes helps, especially in the initial slight embarrassment. I will discuss various projects.

Such as...

Last year I had a large number of foam-rubber genitalia prepared for me by an advertising firm. These were bright pink and varied in size from two feet to six in length, and from a few inches to several yards in circumference. The order was placed on a Monday after a weekend of planning and sketching; on Thursday the genitalia were ready; and on Friday I set out for Niagara Falls with them packed away in my trunk. When I opened the trunk later, at the hotel, the genitalia expanded – virtually exploded – out in my room, filling it. Some had got tangled together, like fingers in doughnuts. That evening I fought my way through the foam to go out and walk among the people, talking to many and asking questions. And the next morning, when the sun was gleaming on the water, I walked with my trunk to the top of the Falls and floated my collection of vast foam genitals down towards all the people below: they bobbed and raged on the water.

Or. I will have a simulacra head made of intelligent clay – in my image precisely, though perhaps a touch more worldly, without the elusive pale delicacy of my own features. With great patience I will teach this head to say Yes, and I will keep it in a wooden box, a box of dogwood, on my left shoulder. Whenever I am asked a question requiring response, I will reach up across my chest and open the door to this box. The head will open its eyes, say Yes – and I will shut the door.

I will train crickets to function as metronomes and place one with every violinist in the world, thus restoring natural order to contemporary music.

By lies and deceit I have caused the Atlantic and Pacific Oceans to become jealous of one another; already they are creeping across America towards a confrontation. Frantically I have this morning cabled the Dead Sea, entreating it to intervene. Which it will.

And she listens. Even as lorries load cans in the alley and roll away, scraping long grooves in the bricks on each side, as the photographers shyly cover their lenses with their hands, as the waiters come and go, replacing dishes, bringing fresh flowers in vase after vase, the clack-clack of them in their rubber shoes. She listens.

And I tell her again, does she understand: "I am a ruined man. This is all I have left. And this, I offer to you." We sit for several minutes listening to corks pop off bottle after bottle around us, like children pulling fingers out of puffed cheeks. They have worked a long time for this; we are at last together. When I look at them, they raise their glasses towards us in celebration. Quickly, more bottles are brought in. A serving cart full of jangling green and clear, that hums and glides too slowly in front of the trotting waiter. More corks, soda, bubbles cascade into glasses, cubes of ice pop up like fishheads and the bubbles resemble their eyes. Me straight in the chair with a high head talking. Admiring how she maneuvers the delicate machinery of eggcup and spoon.

When I am finished she calls softly for the table to be cleared. With a wave of her hand, and light winks in the rings. The band stops and all is quiet as the waiters come and depart with full arms. I am finished. The lights go up, a few people stand for a better view.

She sits straight. So straight like a Cézanne cypress, and hardly anyone breathes now as, smiling, she moves back in her chair and adjusts the top of her body. We hear the gentle, crisp sound of her skirts...

Finally I lift my head out of my wet hands. There is little energy left, in me.

And now there are cheers, calls of approval, relief. She is smiling. Staring straight into my eyes and nothing moves. The green folds of her skirt are pulled back, arranged around her waist and legs like a monster lettuce, and there on the veined-marble table, square in the center by my own, she has put her foot. Her tiny foot is offered, there.

And on it, the most exquisite black shoe.

How's Death?

 Their first intimation of serious trouble was when Dave and Barb named the baby Death.

"Well, of course we *had* hoped you'd carry on your father's name," Beatrice said on the other line.

"O Mom, he'll still be a Dante and all that," Barb said, then giggled. "Sorry. They gave me some shots. I'm still kind of floating around up here."

"Peach jello," Dave said.

"What?"

"You said you felt as though you were suspended in a vat of warm peach jello."

"I *did?*" More giggles.

"Everybody's okay then?" Mr. Dante asked.

"Peachy," Barb said, and dropped the phone.

"We're all fine, Dad," Dave said. "All three of us."

"Have you seen her?" a fifth voice asked. "Has she been there? Why won't you tell me?"

"We were just going to have a nice cup of hot chocolate and go on to bed," Beatrice said. "I wanted to wait up for news from you but Daddy said no."

"Getting in much golf, Dad?"

"Any day the sun doesn't belly up, Dave. Went out this morning with a lung doctor, young guy, new in town. First hole, his beeper goes off and he's gone maybe twenty minutes then comes back and says, God, I hope she makes it. A couple holes later it's squealing again. He comes back and tells me: I lost one, D. Not much longer and he's gone again. Gotta get over to the hospital, he says when he comes back that time. Sorry."

"You just don't know how much I love her," the fifth voice said. "If you did, you wouldn't be doing this."

"We had a new caddy. Terrible child – from the college. Kept quoting Marx to me. Great shoulders, awful manners."

"Barb wanted me to ask if you've been making your regular check-ups, Dad."

"Every month, like clockwork."

"And taking your medicines?"

"Haven't missed a dose."

"No problems?"

"Haven't felt better since I can remember."

There was a pause. Far back in the wires they could hear music. In Minnesota a moth flew against the window again and again. In Texas a gravel truck started up a long incline.

"You're sure nothing's wrong, Dave?" Mr. Dante said after a while.

"Nothing. Everything's fine…great. Mom still on the line?"

"She's gone on up to bed."

"Well, Barb did want me to ask you something. She was wondering if it would be okay for her to come home for a while, Dad. Just a visit, of course."

"She's always welcome at home, Dave, both of you know that. But her home should be *there* now."

"And it is."

"I see." Birds had taken over the newspaper box below the mailbox on its post beside the road; he wondered how long ago that had happened. "You two are having problems."

"Minor stuff, Dad. You know how it is sometimes. It'll pass. But do you think we could keep Mother out of all this? She worries enough as it is. Barb just needs some time alone. Some time away."

"What about the baby? You have to think about that baby now."

"He'll be staying with me…It's okay, Dad, really. I've taken courses and everything. Death and I'll do great together."

"I can't live without her. I really can't," the fifth voice said.

"What I keep thinking about is the courage it takes, Dad."

"To visit her family?"

"No…Things don't stay simple very long, do they?"

"They never are, Dave. But you tell Barb to come on whenever she wants to. And if she does, then you two take good care of yourselves and each other until she gets back. We love you all, Mother and I."

"I know you do, Dad. We all love you. We always will."

"And you call me anytime, Dave. Anything I can do, you let me know."

"Thanks, Dad."

"I'll be talking to you."

"Do you hear someone?" the fifth voice said. "Is there someone else on this line?"

Mr. Dante hung up the phone and stood for a moment in a wedge of moonlight before going upstairs. In bed his wife turned to him and nestled.

"How's Death?" she asked.

"He's fine," Mr. Dante said.

An Ascent of the Moon

His longest relationship, it began over two years ago.

There had been a youthful marriage at age nineteen, a union which wandered about, in and out of various apartments and abandonments, like a movie heroine searching some castle's cavernous hallways and chambers for an outside doorway. But with all that coming and going, the marriage had been patchy and disjunctive at best, and anyway was more than twenty years past.

There followed a six-year affair (using words loosely, which, tacitly, they always insisted upon) with a woman who worked as an agricultural advisor in Africa and returned to Dallas two or three times a year on what were essentially layovers.

In December two years ago he had come across the apartment during an evening walk in the university area. He didn't know why he took notice of the to-let sign, but stood there only a moment, glancing about him at the two-storey houses, each distinct in overall form but identical in detail, doorways and material, before mounting the stoop to inquire. He was shown the room by a youngish woman whose already pale skin was blanched in patches as though randomly daubed with bleach. She wore a denim wrap-around skirt and a man's blue oxford dress shirt falling well below her knees and extending so far beyond her hands that it gave her a vaguely simian look.

The apartment consisted of two rooms tenuously connected by a shoulder-wide hallway which without at all changing its nature suddenly turned downward to become a stairway. Rooms and hallway together comprised a false half-storey, unperceived from outside the house, carved from attic and second-floor space.

One room was afterthought (or afterbirth, as he first thought upon seeing it), a windowless parallelogram too narrow save at the far end to be of much use.

The other, running the house's full length, was less than three yards deep, and along the side, opposite the doorway, ranged a motley of windows of every conceivable form and size – picked up at a bargain, or as surplus, perhaps. Even at this time of late evening, his favorite, neither quite dark nor yet quite light, but something forever in between, something unnameable, unknowable, the room was rich with light. Two ancient trees dipped in from either side and at a distance obscured all but one of the windows. Through this, he saw an expanse of the house opposite: two oversize windows and within them a bedroom, dimly lit, predominantly pink and white.

He moved in a week later, heaving his few possessions up the narrow stairs on his back like a snail. Long ago he had vowed to own nothing that could not be broken down easily for transport or abandoned without regret. In just over an hour furnishings were reassembled, housewares set up and out, clothing, toiletries, books and tapes put away.

That first evening, relocation accomplished, he stood drinking coffee and looking through the chink in the trees. The drapes over there were closed. Once he thought he saw someone moving around behind them, touching gently at their backs, but decided it was only his imagination – or the wind, perhaps.

The drapes remained closed, and he had come to believe the house unoccupied (it was, after all, a neighborhood of students and young families quick to move on) when one evening after his bath, standing as yet undressed near the windows, he looked up and saw the drapes open. A woman of his age or perhaps a bit older stood there, to all appearances watching him through the trees. Slowly her hand reached towards the window. The drapes closed.

The following evening, at the same time, he emerged from his bath and immediately looked up to see the drapes once again open. Tonight, however, the room was unlit, and in the half-dark he could make out only the shape of her, see enough to confirm only that she was again there, again watching.

It continued this way for some time. He would emerge from his bath, at first wearing a robe, later without, and find her there in the window, waiting. They would stand watching as darkness fell. She would reach out and close the drapes.

His days began to gather around these encounters. Whatever those days held (and in truth they held little: students and classes had long since lost any appeal they once may have had), he was at the apartment each evening. The pretense of a shower soon passed. He simply stood by the window and removed his clothes.

Then one evening as he stood there peering across, trying to make out some detail, any detail, in the window opposite, her room suddenly filled with light. He saw her clearly, all but her face, which remained in shadow. She held out her hand, touched softly with its back at the back of the window, and began to remove her own clothes. Only when they were gone (and they went ever so slowly) did she reach out again, to close the drapes. Pulling his blinds closed, he found that he was shaking.

Thereafter, opening his blinds at the proper time, he would see her drapes also opening. Some evenings she would be in nothing but a terry housecoat, others in long skirt and sweater or jeans, once in a formal gown many years out of fashion.

One day then, leaving for a late-afternoon class in first-year Greek, he stepped onto the sidewalk to find a woman standing there before the house opposite, speaking with the postman. Briefly their eyes met, though neither gave any sign of recognition.

That night he waited at the window, looking across at a dark, shrouded window. He believed that he had lost her and did not think he could go on without her. No: he knew that he could not.

For three nights he stood waiting, nibbled at by imagination, sorrow, devastating loss. And when, on the fourth, he opened his blinds and saw drapes parting there in that far window, blood careened wildly inside him and he put his hand on the windowsill to steady himself. Her own hand moved between her legs. Her body twitched and swayed at the end of it. Her eyes never left him.

That night it rained, and afterwards a brilliant yellow moon rose into the sky. For hours he walked gleaming streets. Primitives have always afforded the moon great powers, he thought. Romance, mystery, madness, passion. And any hospital or emergency service will tell you how a full moon calls forth new birth, domestic violence, wave after wave of bodies violated by knives, guns, collisions.

In such a world, he thought, how rare, how very pure and inviolable, was a love like his own.

I Saw Robert Johnson

Let me explain.

I'm an insomniac, you see. Not the kind that has trouble getting to sleep, because three minutes after my head's down, I'm out, but the kind that has trouble staying so: at two or half-past three I'm up and wide-eyed, prowling around the efficiency like a werewolf.

So it was particularly surprising to wake this morning and discover that it was already light outside – that I had slept the night through for the first time in many years. I lay listening to birds sing, the slam of doors across the street, a weather report from my neighbor's radio.

I turned on my side and something leaf-light fell onto my lower lip. I touched it with a finger and the finger came away with a brownish smudge. I rubbed a palm against my cheek and that too was reddish-brown. It was blood, old blood. I swung out of bed then and stood in front of the mirror on the closet door nearby. My entire face was covered with it. Like the facials women get, like makeup base, like warpaint or a mask. There were spatters elsewhere, on my chest, legs and feet, but mostly it was on my face. And a long line tracing the descent of breastbone to pudenda. My hands, apparently, had been washed clean.

Perhaps a few words concerning where I live now, and how I came to be here.

My wife, tolerant, compassionate being that she was, had finally told me to get it together or get out, and so I had, taking a garage apartment within walking distance of both my old house (for tradition's sake) and the university (which had an outstanding collection of old blues records). Across the street is a daycare center, and each morning I sit by the window watching shapely young women deliver their children, opera glasses which have known the soaring Valkyries and shared Carmen's pitiable death now focused on bouncing bosoms, long legs in high heels, waggling buttocks. At a distance, every woman is erotic.

So many people fear being alone. But if you cannot be alone, you cannot know who you are. Listen: this culture conspires to make such essential solitude impossible. Perhaps it fears the individual; certainly the individual has reason to fear *it*.

This place is a dump, one in which the blues records checked out from the school's library seem quite at home. Turning off the lights at night I can hear the roaches begin their peregrinations. Dragging their spurred feet across Bessie Smith's "Empty Bed Blues," or mounting the minute summits of Lonnie Johnson's "Careless Love." I have cleaned and cleaned without result. The odor of mildew and carbon monoxide clings to every corner and crevice; spiders and crane-flies perch like dull thoughts on the walls.

There were on my body no cuts, no wounds to explain all this blood. And I had no memory of the night, only a vague remembrance of dreaming: trees with the face of my wife, grass mowed down that spoke in the voice of my daughter, a parliament of fowls done up in tight skirts and unbuttoned shirtwaists.

The women had begun dropping off children, and I stood at the window nude, my face blood-smeared, wondering what would happen if they should see me. But they did not. Always first the blonde with the pastel sweatsuits and tiny waist. Then the beautiful Latin girl with straight, crow-black hair almost to her knees, always in skirt and jacket. Then the one with impossibly long legs; the pony-tailed redhead who always looked so unhappy; the woman with short brown hair who was always still putting on makeup in the rearview mirror as she pulled away. I know them all, and could not step away from the window until the morning rituals were done. The prettiest of them all, though, a tiny Vietnamese woman, perfectly formed, did not come today.

I brewed a pot of tea and sat at the desk staring out into the yard and drinking tea slowly, cup after cup. The powerful winds of past days had at last blown themselves out and only a mild breeze remained of them. After a time I realized that the lizard I'd been watching run here and there was actually chasing birds; it would wait in the grass until birds settled, then dash towards them, rippling silver in the sunlight, until they flushed and flew away. The lizard did this again and again. I have no idea why.

I will not turn on the radio, I thought. There will be horrible news. There is always horrible news. A tractor-trailer has plunged from an embankment, crushing a bus filled with schoolchildren. A man without food for a week has killed and eaten his neighbor's dog. A woman and daughter living in a house nearby were killed during the night, cut to pieces in their beds. A young Vietnamese was found dead at her apartment early this morning by a friend, murdered. That sort of thing. I will sit here and drink tea, at ease with the world, and then I will call them.

But there was no answer, as you know.

I had not realized so much time had passed, but soon (or so it seemed) the women began picking up their children and I still sat as I had that morning. Watching through the opera glasses as the blonde woman's buttocks and breasts swung freely under the turquoise fabric, I began suddenly to tremble. When they were all gone, I got up and put on some Ma Rainey, stood looking at myself again in the mirror. I tried to imagine what it was like to be black in the Thirties, the rage and hatred you were always having to shove back down inside, shut away again and again, until it finally bubbled to the surface in the blues. In the terrible ache that's become all I can feel now. I put on some Son House, remembering the blonde woman moving underneath her clothes, a rhythm like the earth's itself, like the rise and fall of Son House's moan, like a lizard in the grass. I played the records one after another, some of them twice, and by then it was dark. The drapes closed over my face in the glass, watching.

I drew a hot bath and lay in it for a long time, adding hot water now and again by turning the tap on with my toes. Then I splashed water onto my face and the blood began to come away, swirling out into the water like rust. Yes, *rust.* I sat in the tub and watched it spin off into the drain.

After that I stood staring at the closed drapes. Behind them I could see all those women moving around still, their breasts and hands brushing against the back of the drapes. I could see gin-soaked Bessie Smith bleeding to death on a Mississippi highway. I saw Robert Johnson huddled in a corner, his back to me, singing about his hellhound.

Men's Club

No one remembers now whose idea it was, perhaps it came to all of them at the same time, they all saw her every day, and when they go down into the old room, or just one of them goes, into that room with sweating walls and the stench of butane where the girl lies in her chains, those sharp, darting eyes of hers and the smell of her too, a mix of fear, endless rut and blood, the smell of the dirt floor in her too, and she stands and waits, smiling, always smiling, never drawing away whatever they do, whatever one of them does, they realize they have forgotten the name she certainly must once have had.

The men are much kinder to their wives and daughters now. At their work they prosper. Meeting by chance on the stairs they will relate high profits, a new position, political aspirations, mergers, though always as they approach the end of the stairs they fall, as though by common, though unspoken agreement, silent.

No one has missed the idiot girl, or inquired after her. Of course, there was only the old man who'd taken care of her, at one time he had run the mill and had remained living there, wheel and building rotting out from under, and with him dead no one else was likely to concern himself, concern herself, with the poor creature.

It does not occur to them to wonder what she feels, if she feels, she is smiling, always smiling, and cries only when, whatever they do to her, whatever one of them does, they leave. Perhaps she is sixteen, certainly no more than that, with large breasts gone puffy with rough use and covered with scars from the nicks of teeth and nails. Her ribs protrude under those breasts, making them appear even larger, and her skin is a waxy yellow. Several of the ribs have been broken, many of the teeth now are gone, and the bush between her legs is mostly worn away or has been pulled out, piece by piece, by probing fingers.

For a long time, at first, the little room was in almost continual use. One of them had set up a cask of wine and plastic cups on a table just at the base of the stairs by the door, and here they would, upon arriving and discovering the room already in use, wait their turn. Some brought books, magazines or work from the office in monogrammed attaches, for conversation, even upon those occasions when several waited together, was never undertaken. Each sat somewhat turned away from the others, wrapped in his own work, his own waiting, own wants. Through a narrow window at ground level, at every time of day, it seemed, a light as opaque and unsavory as dishwater poured down on them.

Gradually fewer of them will be found in the outside room, and at increasing intervals; the cask will be again drained and this time go unreplaced. The flood become river, stream, brook, pond, draught. Finally the girl lies alone in her chains, waiting.

It is the wives and daughters, of course, who will bear the burden of their abjuration.

Perhaps the girl (whose name, I will tell you now, is Barbara) somehow will remain alive down there. Perhaps at every creak of the ancient, empty house above her, she looks to the door and stands (as long as she *can* stand) expectantly, smiling, always smiling. Perhaps on the wind at night she hears the names of her nameless lovers, saying them over and over, remembering them, in her tongueless mouth.

Others

The best part was when he got a new letter, walking back from the mailbox with it, reading it over and over, the possibilities that crowded in on him then. A few were so very powerful, so redolent of potential, that he never answered them. Sometimes he would put a letter, unopened, on his desk and force himself to wait an hour, even two, before reading it. Then he would read each line many times before going to the next. All during the day he'd be pulling out one or another of them, savoring their individual flavors, trying (though never successfully) to capture those first magic moments.

This was all he used the desk for now. Ever since he could remember, he had wanted to be a writer. And with his wife's sudden death (a stroke at age 34, then pneumonia) he had quit his job and set himself up as a novelist, living off the insurance money. The first novel had been about her and was titled *Julia*, her name; it went unpublished. There came then a string of books: mysteries, science fiction, teen romances, pornography, each completed in precisely thirty days. A few were published, each by a different house, and his royalty statements showed him owing more than the money advanced him. He attended college for a time, taking mainly philosophy courses; made a stab at learning Spanish; worked briefly in a bookstore catering to collectors.

He discovered *The Pen* two years after Julia died, about the time he was writing his last book, a serious novel about a man who moves into a new apartment and gradually discovers (or becomes convinced) that his predecessor was an agent of some sort, a man more of shadow than substance whose whole identity was assumed, manufactured – then abandoned for another again and again, endlessly.

The Pen was a biweekly "alternative" newspaper devoted chiefly to the arts and left-wing journalism. But each issue contained five or six pages of classified advertisements grouped under such headings as Women Seek Men, Men Seek Women, Gay, Miscellaneous. He became an instant convert; subscribed, but haunted newsstands for early copies; responded to every plausible ad with lengthy letters in perfect handwriting. Certain things led him to discount automatically any advertisement: undue emphasis on appearance or wealth, statistics (age, measurements, weight, salary, height), puns, any reference to a 10, the words "sensitive," "gentle" and "professional," use of song titles, undue length, poor grammar. There still remained, however, a large number, and he answered them all.

Each morning he sat down with his second cup of coffee and again read through recent arrivals.

> Dear John,
>
> Thank you for answering my ad. I'm "Farmer's Daughter," all alone out here. I was glad to hear about your childhood on the farm in Iowa, how much that's meant to you. If you'd like, maybe we could get together over a homecooked meal some night and I could show you the place.

Not too many more possibilities to explore there; it was pretty obvious. He put that one in the dead file.

> Carl,
>
> Yes, it *is* a lonely world and we *should* do everything we can to help one another – *must*. I hope very much that when you return to "the States" from Central America,

you will write me. As I told you in the last letter, I am overweight and not very pretty, I think, but under the right man's hand I could be anything he wished.

Often after the third or fourth letter he would call, not uncommonly talking two or three hours, but then, after that, would not write again. He changed his post-office box frequently. All we truly want, and can never have (he had decided some time ago), is to know another person, to bridge this awful solitude we're locked into. Power, influence, knowledge of every arcane, recondite sort, our impulses to art, sex – all were merely analogs, pale reflections of that simple basic, unfulfillable drive. Instinctively he knew that with his letters he approached as close as one really ever could to other people. And certainly he knew that the rest would be messy: awkward pauses, inferred obligations, misunderstandings, rejection.

David,
It sounds as though a single dip in your lake might wash off all the dirt of previous relationships.

Carlos,
I just want someone to hold me sometimes. I am a career woman with three degrees, own my own business, play aggressive racquetball.

Hi Jonathan!
I'm "41, Mensa member." Want to push some pawns? QP – QP4!

Once he'd gone so far (she had a lovely voice, and her interests overlay his own exactly) as to arrange a meeting. From afar he had watched her arrive, look about, seat herself and order tea, read for a while and finally depart. He was terrified the whole time. She did not seem unduly surprised or upset. He watched men's eyes following her out the door.

Dear Elizabeth,

I have read your ad with great interest, noting in particular your love of cats and Bach. As it happens, at the time I first came across your ad I was sitting on the patio, my own Siamese curled in my lap and the initial strains of the Air for G-string drifting out from the house into the gathering twilight – surely an omen, if one could believe such things.

This is all so new to me, I don't know what to write, what you expect to hear. I am in my late 30's, a widower, not bad looking but no prize either. I suppose that my strong points are kindness, caring, concern. I can recite the whole of Chaucer in middle English and tell *Beowulf* from Grendel's point of view.

Debra,

Since you ask, my favorite movie is the first *Robin Hood*, because it has that scene where someone (a beautiful girl?) says, You speak treason! And Robin responds: Fluently.

Judith,

I'm sorry, but I am not *allowed* to tell you about what I do for a living; I can only say that it is boring, repetitious, often difficult. Many days I feel that I no longer belong to the human race. Of course I am quite well paid.

Around noon he always broke off for a while, brewed another pot of coffee, had a light lunch of cheese and fruit or soup if some was left over from the previous evening. He would browse randomly among favorite books, stories and poems: "Heart of

Darkness," Gerard Manley Hopkins, later Yeats, *Moby-Dick*, most of Hawthorne, "Entropy," Robbe-Grillet. Frequently he thought of the fascination for masks in Greek tragedy, romantic and gothic fiction, Durrell's *Alexandria Quartet*.

> Dear Sammi,
> Like you I am tired of games, tired of bodies that won't quit and minds that have to be jumpstarted.

> June,
> It is evening. Frogs on the pond not far away do Hoagy Carmichael songs you've never heard. From my garden seat all I can see are trees, grass, sky. All about me there is a low whisper.

And other declaiming the nonimportance of money, Marxist theory, the supremacy of art, how hard it was to meet people and how hard they were once met. Only in these letters could he, did he, truly live.

One in particular, however, bothered him. It was so adaptive, so labile, like the letters he himself composed so carefully on the pegs of others' dreams. He thought of the famous Marx Brothers mirror routine, Harpo (or was it Chico?) suspecting that the doorway was not in truth a mirror but unable to prove it, the "reflection's" movements never deviating from, or lagging behind, his own. Perhaps this letter was from a female counterpart. Perhaps there were many like himself, living submerged in this system of correspondence like deepsea animals, never coming up for air.

At five or so he would put the letters aside and have dinner on the patio, generally soup and fruit or a simple stew followed with bread (which he baked himself) and cheese. But this time he had brought with him her latest letter.

Dear John,

I am so comfortable writing to you, as though we've been friends a long time. Truly, I wonder if you are not the one I've waited for all these lonely years. We have so very much in common – more than you realize. Please write again soon or call me. I am waiting.

He finished his meal and sat watching a squirrel leap from tree to tree. Wind ferried in a smell of dust and the sun rolled across moving clouds. He thought of the bouncing ball over song lyrics in "short subjects" that once accompanied all movies. Nothing like that now. Nothing but ads now, ads and future attractions. Sex, violence, power, war, wealth.

After a time he stood and walked to the edge of the patio, looking out into the thick growth of oak, ivy, kudzu, honeysuckle. He knew that he would write to her again. He knew that he would call then, and just how her voice would sound. He knew that he would talk and talk – talk for an hour, two, three if she would listen – trying to hold off the inevitable moment there was no more to say: the moment the phone fell back into its cradle, taking her away from him forever.

Jane Crying

This is my wife in the blue window crying. And my son in the room behind her playing with his Christmas toys. As you can see, she is wearing only a delicate yellow bra and even at this distance you can tell how soft and smooth her brown skin will be. When you touch it. That first time.

As I recall, we met while skydiving. I came out of the plane after her, fell free until I was just above the silk mushroom of her parachute, then pulled the cord of my own kit. I believe we discussed Kant on the way down. That is to say, the categorical imperative.

But she is not crying. She is laughing. They are all laughing. Jane, Pam, Barbara, Pat, Chris. They are all together in bed. Happy and laughing. They are drawing straws tonight. Pam draws the short one. The others use their own straws to tease her erogenous zones, of which she has more than her fair share. This is to excite her sexually. So she will be ready. When I come. At the height of her passion.

My wife is sitting in an expensive Danish chair. It is her parents' chair. In her parents' home. She is sitting before the fireplace in which they burned the gift wrappings last night but there's no fire now. Only the light on the snow. The light of the moon, a clean cold light. She is trying to keep from thinking about thinking about crying. About me.

For years then I didn't see her. Till one day, skindiving off Bermuda, and a shark approached. As we had been well taught, we swam together directly towards the shark and thumped it on the nose, whereupon it fled. Naturally this shared experience created an instant bond between us. She invited me to her cabana for a drink and we talked over old times. Later we dined together and she introduced me to my son. The following day we were married.

This is my wife at a party with someone. She is wearing a dazzling low-cut Neiman Marcus gown and has somehow contrived to have breasts. Her hair is blonde and she is wearing a fall, piled and twined into an intricate coiffure atop her head. There are pink pearls resting against her skin, the soft brown skin at the base of her neck. She is smiling and slightly drunk on Brandy Alexanders. Perhaps this is not my wife at all.

Kate. Joanna. Hilary. Pam. Carol. Crystine. Renée. Wynn.
56 Ridgemount Gardens. 141 East 13th. 6 rue de Tournon. 221 Camden High Street. Houston and Delancey. Cracow. Juarez. Harlem. Rio. Milford.

She hasn't heard from me for several years and received this morning a copy of *Certains*, a collection of poems written in French published last year in Paris and dedicated to her. Á Jane, á jamais. The first section is titled "Poésies pour la mort." She has been trying all day to read it. Now she is reading one of the books I gave her. *L'Écume des jours*. She reaches the end, cries, reads it again. She is reading the last chapter with her eyes closed. Tears are coming out from under the lids.

Marc. Gary. Ted. John. Terry. André. Marek. Bob.

5430 Wateka Drive. 331 Harvard Street. 18 Orchard Street. 6918 Philadelphia Avenue. Dallas. Cambridge. Boston. Mexico City. Washington. Dallas.

Now she is crying because she is in a white gown at a wedding. Because we are being married again. My son is the best man.

She is crying again. Our son has left to find me. He believes I am in Paris and has flown there to bring me back. He is 12.

This is my wife at her first one-man show in a Boston gallery. She has lost weight and is wearing a trousersuit. Her hair is black. She is wearing glasses. She is beautiful. She is crying because they are buying all of her paintings.

Jane. Gail. Cambridge.

Jim. Julio. Argentina.

She takes the news quite well. *Missing in action.* This is my wife in the blue window crying. It was the least I could do.

Allowing the Lion

It was in early April, on a day whose radiant weather they remember well, that the monster came to live with them. Its manners were excellent. It would not hear of discomforting them further, for surely its mere presence in their home was imposition enough, it said, and declined their offer of the second bedroom, bedding down instead in a corner of the livingroom and attending (whatever those were) to its own needs. It did eat with them, however, each time leaving at its place, despite continued protestations, a five-dollar bill.

At first they turned away, but then found themselves drawn back and would sit watching the monster's vast head and its hands that manipulated so adroitly and with such casual grace the various spoons, forks and knives. It had a particular fondness for soups and freshbaked bread, and was adamantly vegetarian. Some evenings it would tell them amazing stories of its own far land.

For many years they, Kathryn and Karl, had slept in separate rooms. Some weeks after the monster's arrival they moved all their things into the smaller of the two bedrooms, telling themselves that the monster might after all wish to use the other. At night, as they watched the monster eat and upon occasion heard its stories (for it disliked, it said, though in fact there was none without its, monopolizing the conversation), he began to notice that she was

27

looking across the table at him in an old, barely remembered way, and he himself felt stirrings long forgotten. Standing, he would contract the muscles of his stomach, jam a hand into one pocket, lean backwards against his bending spine. She would worry at her hair, take time each morning selecting her clothes and often change them, breathe through the words she said to him.

At the end of the first year the monster spent with them, she awoke one morning to find him sleeping beside her in the narrow bed. Some weeks or months later she awoke to the same surprise, and with his hand, moreover, at her breast. This was repeated many times, neither of them speaking of it, and then came the night that, just after retiring, she heard his feet on the floor, crossing to her, and the wind of the covers lifting, the warm hardness of him behind her, then inside her.

The next morning they looked everywhere for the monster, for their guest, but it was not to be found. There remained only the faint scent of its perfume in the livingroom, a few torn rags in the room's corner, the memory of its eloquently trilled *r*'s.

Only the Words Are Different

1
Pulse

I just looked up and a man fell by my window with his arms waving. (Earlier, my thumb was engaged in moving across the paper like a chicken drumstick. Scratching, scratching.) He seems to have been in a great hurry, and possibly there was something he wanted to tell me. This may, I realize, have something to do with the scaffolding which grew outside my window during the night; it's out there now, as I write, a wood and steel doily of piping, ladders, planks and pant legs;

the sky shows through
in squares of blue.

I go to the window and there is a crowd below me, a red truck with two white attendants. The man is lying strangely on the pavement; perhaps he is very tired. Pigeons tiptoe down his legs and arms. Snails would be better, but snails are not in season – only strawberries. His mouth is full of strawberries. The red juice dribbles out of his mouth and streams along the pavement.

I wonder what it was that he wanted to tell me? Probably that he loved me.

2

Schlupp-thunkk. Schlupp-thunkk. The wipers mimic a heart. Beating.

Postmortems of parties dead and cold now, passing home in a bouncing car. You here beside me, warm with drinking, soft with sleep in your pumpkin dress that skis off one shoulder and slides along your leg. The child in your lap. Shapeless in her bundle of flannel.

— like it'll snow forever. And our Fiat crunches through the crust of that snow. The motor, in third, hums and whirrs. Thinking of our Ford gathering snow on the salvage yard. In the back seat now there are the remains of two pheasants and a bottle of brandy. The brandy rolls and clatters against the oven pan, rolls in its nest of birds' bones and greasy dressing. Snow stipples the flat grey air, slurs the streets. I smoke the last cigarette and watch for ice. Guilt in small actions, always. The heater growls.

Who was that girl?

I pass the cigarette to you, you drag once and hand it back. The tip is wet now. Of course.

The sexy one. You consider her, try to remember other qualities she may have had. Long hair, boots. The one who kept drinking the brandy.

I shrug. Undergrad, I think. Light from an oncoming car catches in my eyes, trapped under the ridges, supraorbital—as you say, like Pueblo cliffs, a moderately effete baboon. (And you…you have sat on those ledges and watched a world, the world in front, the world behind them…lived on the edge, looking.)

Painter?

That's the guy she was with. Workshop, I think. Supposed to be very good. She has a novel coming out next year, from Harper.

In your class?

Too obvious, Jane. The brandy, or real annoyance? I shift into second to take a curve. The wipers are tossing snow away from the windshield. We are tossing away time. To buy our way home.

No. Not many of the writers are interested in Pope, they mostly go for modern lit. I've told you all that before.

The baby has crapped in its sleep and the smell fills the car. You reach for the cigarette, draw, encounter filter and throw it out, leaving the window a little open. You twist and rummage through your pockets; skirt, sweater, coat. I thought I had a pack of Salems somewhere…

We smoked them.

So: that sideways glance. A measured reprehension. A truck comes towards us, puffing chimney, cab outlined in small red lights. A huge interstate rig. We're out of the city, coming onto open road. I shift to fourth and see your face in the truck's lights. How many times, these five years, this same moment? The Fiat takes the curve and starts up a hill, dropping speed. Touching the shift, I almost touch your knee but you pull away. The road drops steadily into the darkness, the vacuum, behind us. The lights spread out in front of us, a dull flash-lightning inside the fog, that goes on and on.

Look! but we've passed it, whatever it was.

What…

A Styrofoam snowman. Someone has a goddamn Styrofoam snowman in their yard…

O *shit*! A Styrofoam snowman.

If another truck, even a car, came by, I might see you crying. But nothing else passes, we're alone on the road. I can only hear the sound of your breath in the dark. Finally you lean forward and shut off the heater.

How much further?

A few miles.

O.

3

Have you ever noticed how books accumulate around you? Like clouds. You don't remember putting them there, or buying them (and if you *had* bought them, you'd have put them on the coffee table, or a shelf, or perhaps beside the bed). And they couldn't have come through the mail slot; it's too small. The post office doesn't deliver. You never enter it: the Draft Board is just upstairs. But they go on accumulating, even now that you know, like clouds.

Then one day there appears on your desk – a surprise beside your morning coffee – this memo advocating the extinction of poems (though a few would be maintained in cages, well-fed and cared for, for the children to see; to which they might toss an occasional left-over letter, partly eaten or melted to a shapeless mess in their warm hands; perhaps an occasional colon or dash; an adjective, apostrophe). You quickly add your name – recalling it, letter by letter, as you write – to the already formidable list. This, it occurs to you now, is a petition. You pick it up and the first page comes apart in your hands like a newspaper. It begins to unfold, a very long list indeed. You follow the names through the study, library, den, kitchen, living room, dining room, up three flights of stairs to the bedroom. You jump out the window and run, as though you are (in October) flying a kite, and still the petition comes open, unfolds, like panels of toilet paper folded front to back, back to front, front to back. Each is stamped in blue *Property of the British Government* and you realize now that this was stolen from the Tate, more precisely from one of the toilet booths on the bottom floor by the cafeteria, behind the Trova and would-be Michelangelo virgin.

You run, you run, you're out of breath. Finally, in New Jersey, you reach the end of the list. It began with the names of several well-known artists (painters, sculptors, ceramists, film-makers, mixed mediasts) and ends with the signature of the local cub reporter. The only names missing are those of the poets themselves – though a few of them, too, have signed. Under pressure, one presumes. Of their wives, publishers, bankers, typewriters, cigarettes, "humor". All the way back across mitred New Jersey, New York and Pennsylvania, you search for your name but are unable to find it, even in Philadelphia. But you *have* considered removing it and this, like the poetry itself, is a noble gesture. You are sure of that, at least...

Over dinner I explain all this to you, my wife, and your new friend Harrison. It apparently means little to you, but Harrison feigns interest quite well. And I like him. I feel myself attracted to this strange, quiet man. But let me warn you, Darling: *his name was not on that list!*

4
Story

They are in love. They go to the beach at Brighton and she is disappointed, there are only rocks, where is the sand. The Camden Town Zoo. Shopping together at Heal's. The East and West for curry, Westbourne Grove (Notting Hill). Baby elephant. Theatre closed – seats outside for sale, want them, can't find anyone to ask. They return to Portobello Road and, stomachs rumbling from the Madras (this, like the sound of wind in the pastiche-Corbusier elephant house), make love. She wants "your child". Sadly watching him roll the rubber down over his penis, thinks of discarded peacock feathers lying on ground at zoo, they climax (him 3, her 2). Nothing is ever said. He returns with her to America (on the boat, his birthday, she has him lean his arms against the upper bunk and masturbates him, slowly). They take a flat just outside New York. Strain of isolation, his disorientation, intimations of an affair apart from her. Their love, always silent, is now proclaimed in words. The words distort, fictionalize, lead them each into "false" emotions; they are farther apart with each day, each word (she still wants his child). He finally leaves in the middle of the night, after a (rationalized) argument – the words – over sex. Three days later she receives a small package. No name, no return address, postmark Grand Central Station. She opens the package, which is beautifully gift-wrapped, and takes out what is inside. Holds it up to the light of the kitchen window: precise visual description. A rubber, the nipple filled with semen, a knot tied just above it. Title: *Love Letter*.

5

MOLLY keeps a cockroach. It lives in a cage made of Japanese matchsticks, the size of a child's shoebox, floor covered with a jiggerful of sawdust. It lives on charcoal which it extracts from cigarette filters dropped into its cage by Molly and her lovers, rolling the residue of paper into tiny neat balls to store in one corner of the cage. When Molly mates, it climbs up the side, crawls upside-down halfway out across the top, then drops down into the litter and starts up the side again – faster and faster, again and again. Finally it drops down onto its back and lies there in the sawdust, exhausted, moving its legs slowly, like eyelashes.

Afterwards Molly stands by the cage telling us, The roach is a dead end, it hasn't changed in a handful of thousands of years.

Later the roach will ascend to the light fixture and cry there for the crumbling dry bodies of flies. When Molly climbs on a chair to bring it down, it will stare at her with its one cold black eye, it will wave one leg frantically in her face. *J'accuse, J'accuse.*

THE MAYOR has declared war on roaches, believing common cause will bring us together; restore esprit, order. Contraceptives have been burned in bonfires on Town Hall Square, people queue outside the compulsory strip shows, the city's water supply is pumped full of aphrodisiacs – and still, it's not enough. No one cares. No one, frankly, gives a damn. Anomie and entropy. The birthrate still declines, the city collapses into itself. Stronger measures are required, the Mayor declares from the top of the Town Hall steps (the sun on his skull; the smell of burnt rubber, burning plastic), We *must* act *now*!

Badges came last night, press-gang firemen, to bear Molly's roach away to its execution. She locked the door and shoved things against it – bureaus, bookshelves, the stove – and when they finally broke through, attacked them with shishkebob skewers. She blinded three, ruined another's hand, neatly burst the balloonlike testicles of the last. Holding her, kicking, screaming, against the wall (halls filled with inquisitive Citizens), they took the cage-cover off and discovered that she had (predictably, perhaps) killed the roach herself – with a gold stickpin left behind by one of her lovers – to keep them from getting it.

Molly, 'The stars and the rivers
and waves call you back.'

AND THE CITIZENS, when they return to their flats from gaping and gasping in the hall – what is it that they do? There, in that abject privacy. Contained by those colorful walls.

Syphilis: A Synopsis

The global outbreak of syphilis
and gonorrhea spawned by World War
II came as no surprise to the
medical world.

I've had syphilis in London, in Paris, in Timbuktu, in Istanbul, on the road, in Hong Kong (it fit perfectly), in Delhis old and New. I've had syphilis in Warsaw, in Cracow, in Berlin (twice); in Juarez, in Rio, in Liverpool, in absentia. The most interesting experience I've had with syphilis was in Borneo. There, it takes the form of flying snakes, which drop onto you from the trees. The worst period is between 2 and 6 in the afternoon, especially during the rainy season (March to December). No one escapes. Several tribes consider it a sacred disease, proof of enduring ancestral spirits; for others it is a rite of passage, with coming of age marked from its first inception.

In 1530 an Italian pathologist, Hieronymus Fracastorius, wrote a poem entitled Syphilis Sive Morbus Gallicus, which described the plight of a mythical shepherd lad named Syphilus afflicted with the French disease as punishment for cursing the gods. The poem recognized the venereal nature of the infection and was a compendium of knowledge of the time regarding the disease.

It is common fact that Adolf Hitler had syphilis. So badly was his vision impaired that it became necessary to construct a special typewriter with an inch-high typeface; and from this typewriter came his later speeches, noted for their brevity and compression. Thus is syphilis a primary influence on the course of world events. One authority in fact states that the Great War was fought "to make the world safe for syphilis."

Contracting syphilis, then, affords one a considerable historical perspective, meanwhile serving to make one feel ever more intensely a part of his world.

Among other famous syphilitics are Martin Luther, J.S. Bach, Voltaire, Thomas Aquinas, John Alden, Diogenes, and Pocahontas.

Of the literature dealing with syphilis, *Pinocchio* is, with its obvious symbolism, the best known.

The Colombian school believes that syphilitic infection was endemic in Hispaniola (Haiti) and was subsequently contracted and carried to Europe by Columbus' crew when they returned to Spain following his second voyage.

I have myself known, some of them close friends, 47 syphilitics; I met the latest just this afternoon at the Coolidge Corner Laundromat; others, I have wondered about. (Bob, Tom, Mark, Mike.) Last month a friend and I were walking down or perhaps up 42nd Street. My friend nodded towards an old man with no nose who stood dispensing Scientology bulletins on the corner outside one of several blood banks *(Immediate Payment)*. Syphilis, my friend said. A 12-year-old Puerto Rican came up behind us, unwrapping a new stiletto from lavender tissue the gift shop had set it among. Crabs, he said.

It was in Kansas City that I had this story from a young man met by chance at the out-patient Coke machine:

"So I got this call one day, see. It's summer, and this old biology teacher of mine's calling up to take me to a movie because I was his best student. He's leaving, got a new job. It's with the Health Department and he's going to be working with VD. I'm about fourteen, see. Then later I hear he's been dismissed and I say guess what for – yeah, he was passing out free samples."

Syphilitics are often of such humorous turn of mind.

There is the case of Prince Lentille, who upon learning that he had contracted syphilis, caused every courtesan of the Royal Family to be killed and interred dans les jardins de palais. This is the first record of syphilitic dandelions.

> The first documented outbreak of
> syphilis, or "the great pox,"
> followed the siege of Naples by the
> French in 1494, giving rise to the
> now discounted legend that
> Columbus' men had brought the
> disease back from the New World.

Jane?
Gail?

It is obvious that neither theory
of the origin of syphilis is
entirely satisfactory.

Having suffered for some time from painful boils and difficult urination, a poet went finally to his physician.

You have contracted syphilis, the physician, a writer himself but only of prose, said following a brief examination. Examination consisted of asking the poet to drop his pants. Treatment involved asking the poet to drop his pants *and turn around.*

Not consumption? the poet asked sadly.

Keep trying! the physician said, plunging the needle in deep. He thought of his half-completed novel, waiting at home.

In some cases syphilis is accompanied by a condition known as penicillin shock.

"He who knows syphilis, knows
medicine." (Sir William Osler)

How to Get the Most Out of Your Syphilis
Syphilis Without Fear
The Syphilitic Cookbook
Joysores!
Le Mal anglais
VD: Home Cures
General Paresis and Private Parts

So they gave him the little book with the awful pictures and he promised to read it all. U.S. Government Printing Office. Public Health Service Publication No. 1660. Rubber-stamped on flyleaf and title page:

Compliments of
New York City Dept. of Health
Bureau of Venereal Disease Control
LE 2-4280

That's as far as he gets. Immediately he calls a printer to have a tiny rubber stamp of his own made: Compliments of _____.

Lots of red ink.

From syphilis we learn that *sex is dangerous*.

Syphilis is often shared by husband and wife, much as they share the evening Globe, Johnson's shampoo, their paychecks, a bed, one of his T-shirts, the last scoop of ice cream.

It will be found that syphilis, though most generally introduced outside the marriage parameter, often functions to bring the family unit closer together.

In a recent poll, asked who had syphilis, 26 out of 30 pre-schoolers raised their hands.

While in the dank jungles of the Orient new strains develop, breed profusely and prosper.

"That most democratic of diseases...."

And there is syphilis in Salt Lake City, like clouds. Syphilis storms the ramparts at San Antonio. Syphilis floats raftlike and silently on the river towards Memphis. There is syphilis in Des Moines, there is syphilis in Grand Rapids, there is syphilis in San Jose, syphilis in Forts Worth and Lauderdale. There is syphilis in Oxford, Nice, Toledo. There is no syphilis in Boston.

I've always wanted to go to Boston.

Récits

I used to live with a woman who looked like you. She had large breasts that hung down and rolled across the top of her stomach and she always supported them, the weight of them, with the flat of her arms, hugging herself like a toy bear. Her teeth were even, like tiny ceramic tiles, the color of milky amber. Getting in, out of bed she always kept her legs together.

Afterwards the room seemed so much…larger. As I stood looking at the closed door. I was aware for the first time of the space between things.

Her proportions were always astounding; each day, I discovered them as though for the first time. Her buttocks, the short firmness of her legs, the shallow back and small shelf there – these were not the ones expected, my wife's. They startled.

She disliked my smoking in bed. So afterwards, I would sit in the chair across the room by the window, watching her. The electric heater glowed against the wall and sparkled when I lit cigarettes off it. She wore shiny, round-toed shoes, wrinkled on the top, with buckle-straps going across. And tights, always – I never saw her without tights.

At two or three we would reach up in the dark and it was like shutting doors. I would lie watching her dress, then dress myself. Walk four blocks and find a cab. Back to her husband, who wouldn't ask questions. On the street: You don't take care of yourself, you know. On the street: I'm an abstraction, to you, I could be anyone. I am woman. The thing – perhaps even the quality.

When she was gone, the knives would come out of the mirror like sharks.

Some of us who come to London never drink coffee again.

We are sitting in a Lyons, having tea in the middle of the morning. Somehow (the way I chew my toast?) the talk has got onto the subject of camels.

"One hump or two?"

You will want to know
how I am making
out here in this
city of penetrating light.

I should write you letters
explaining that I am in
fact doing well; how pleasant
it is here, how good jobs
are easily come by, how
beautiful the children are.

These letters would make
you smile, know how I miss
you, make you go look
out your window and looking
for men. In your hands,
with all the scribbling
and erasure, my pressured
hand, they would have
the texture of lettuce leaves.

When we make love she turns her face to the wall, where blond and grey stripes resemble an abstract cypress forest. She puts a knuckle in her mouth, hears my watch ticking by her ear. The heater glows against the wall. Only in the final moments does she turn her face up and open her eyes, watching me. There is a spring coming up through the sheet. And then she says Hmmmm.

Later, we fold a torn sheet several times and lay it like a bandage, a compress, over the spring.

P.S. Indubitably.

Locust husks! Summers (he thinks it was summers) they'd hang askew all over trees, fences, even the side of the house. Light and fragile as fallen leaves, dead spurs caught in the bark, burst in a split along the back. He collected them; he remembers one summer when a whole wall of his room was covered with them. Lined perfectly, all climbing upward, row by row.

Also: figs, fireflies searching for an honest man, the red veins in shrimp.

1. What is the exact nature of their relationship?
    Changeable.
    Is there a word?
    Weighty.

    And is he weary?
    Yes.

    Of?
    Explanations, digressions, rationalizations, endless
    nights of discussion – what should she do?

2. A quality of hers: to live in a maze of possibilities.
    A quality of his: to accept as what he *can* occur, only
    that which *does* occur.
    The first allows great freedom of movement and
    excludes responsibility; the second, similarly,

makes guilt impossible. More and more, it is this
that sustains him.

3.   Him, aware of himself – and her, of him moving
within her.
He has said in his allusive way that together they are long-
legged flies. He tries to explain country music to her.
Finally, as so many times before, he falls back to
Creeley: "it is only in the relationships men
manage, that they live at all."

4.   Where does it end?
On the 52 bus, halfway between Notting Hill Gate and
Marble Arch.

Were there prior signals?
Cabs, for them, assumed a large importance. They
began to read the names on bus panels and wonder
about those places, where they might be.

How did it end?
In argument over the respective merits of various
shampoos.

– Across this page of his notebook (as well as many others,
and all the poems) he has scrawled *HA* a number of times,
H rolling lightly like a valley into the *A*'s hill.

They trade stories about shells.
She used to find in the Florida ocean, floating branches which,
removed, proved to be covered with clam shells, tiny and white and
perfect as teeth.
He once came across a huge pile of shells on the bank of a bay.
Chalky white and crunching to bits when he walked into them.
Bending to look closer, he discovered that each shell was punched
full of round, button-sized holes; what remained were the narrow
spaces around the holes, looking like a patchwork of nose septums.

P.S. I love you.

P.S. I miss you.

P.S. I enjoy mispelling and singing.

She swears that roaches live in the Swiss cheese at this delicatessen; you can see their heads popping out on the hour for a look 'round. At night they chew the soft cheese like the wax in your ears. She points out how very much this cheese resembles sponge – and how roaches, like many deepsea fish, haven't changed in thousands of years. But he doesn't believe her.

He was ill. She learned this from friends and came walking down Portobello Road with cheese and apple juice early one morning. That was the first time they tried to end it.

He has said: It's your freedom makes me do this.

And she: You contain me.

He has a knack for aphorism and she, for conjuring disappointment. Often, sitting beside her, he feels he has been in some obscure way defeated. Her preparation of meals for him, or his for her, has somehow come to be like the running-up of flags. Each morning she goes and brings him things: food, cigarettes, soup, soap, shower attachments. You don't take care of yourself, she says.

At night, in the dark room, they open doors to a few more monads; advance to the next chamber of the nautilus. He begins to perceive new relationships everywhere. An evening sky is the color of kazoos, his brown shoes on the floor are abandoned tanks.

He asks her, What do penises look like? And she answers: mushrooms. One of his favorite foods.

Later she is asleep and he suddenly exclaims, The fish are not afraid!

She starts awake and when he repeats it, this delights her. But he didn't want to repeat it.

– They are in the cab.
  They are going home.

– He to his, her to hers.
  With?

– Platitudes, gratitudes.
  But the age demands an image.

– True.
  Well?

Days later: "The residue of each in all the others." A warm day, with pigeons in the corners, and rain.

P.S. I got your letter today and will write again when I can.

I shall answer rage with outrage; expect you to collect my words in little wood boxes of parsley or sawdust; require that you follow behind, obligatto? No.

Outside, standing by the cab, I hear his shouts, the clatter of things thrown at the floor. The driver and I talk about last night's rain; how it took him two hours to cross town, generally a fifteen-minute trip; how he got a fare to Brighton, ten quid. You come out the door when streetlights are turning from orange to yellow, you are wearing your cantaloupe-color coat, the cab's blue light glints in your glasses.

Now, in the cab, you begin to talk.

"Selling pieces of my life. Am being, in a sense, auctioned off – but this is of course no truer for me than for others. Just that my bids are recorded.

"Publishers, contracts, agents, a grant here, a fellowship there, royalty statements, letters; half for my wife, son, friends.

"There is 10% left. That, I offer to you."

My speech, too much used: Je me retournerai souvent.
Memory is a hunting horn
It dies along the wind

Books, papers and typewriter, flowers in a beer bottle – on his desk.

For him: the texture of the moment, objects in disarray.

For her: a pattern of abstractions.

"I think my period is starting, you may get blood on you."

"That's fine."

"I didn't know. Whether it would matter."

Later, waking in the night, he realizes how participation in the present is always diluted – by memory, by anticipation. He resents this. Against the window and light outside, the flowers are transformed. He is becoming confused. He is terrified of hurting her.

Believe, please, that I understand and appreciate your concern but feel it, upon this occasion, somewhat a waste. By actual count there were fifty-seven people directly concerned with my affairs yesterday; and from every indication the number has risen considerably today.

At the top of this page you'll find a small rendering of two cows facing one another across a field of watercress; this is in the nature of a bonus, on your stock in me.

P.S. All the flagpoles have bloomed to flowers. The air smells of eggshells and coffee grounds. There are meringue nativity scenes in all the eggshells. I am yours.

"The goddamn hot-water heater only heats three cups of water at a time."

"Yeah."

Things in the world: a series. A drawing.
1. Mozart
2. Watermelon
3. Oil derricks
4. Puce
5. Drambuie

Why, he asks, this urge towards capitalization?

She wants to answer but all she can think is *epithesis* – a nonce word. He gives her *micturation* in return and for days, at every opportunity, they are rehearsing one another's words. They often make these trades.

Smoking American cigarettes in London. A bit of chauvinism to contrast his adoption of a British accent, British clothes, British mannerisms, always saying "Sorry." (When she brings an American penny out of her purse he laughs; dollars, though, he can still accept as authentic, unsuspect.)   Five bob a pack: made in Switzerland under American license. To buy them he puts on his best voice, assumes a business air, gets it over with as quickly as possible. He is embarrassed; she loves it.

She begins to recognize lines from Creeley.

> Love comes quietly,
> finally, drops
> about me, on me,
> in the old ways.
>
> What did I know
> thinking myself
> able to go
> alone all the way.

Or:

> Everything is water
> if you look long enough.

His favorite:

> What
> has happened
> makes
>
> the world.
> Live
> on the edge,
>
> looking.

Conversation becomes for them a kind of verbal semaphore. Sentences need never be finished. A word, a pause – and the other is smiling, responding, thoughtful. Perhaps the sentences *couldn't* be completed; perhaps they were begun – formed – in this certainty of communication. Sometimes she wonders. She considers holding back her response, to see.

Toys.

As a child she slept in a bed full of stuffed animals, contorting herself to fit in among them. He once began a poem: We lie down, the menagerie invades our bed.

She doesn't know about gigging frogs, so he tells her. The miniature trident; how he went gigging toads when he was ten, not knowing the difference; how difficult it is to kill a toad (one, he stabbed fifteen times). Then he explains how you can milk a toad using two matchsticks, something his grandmother taught him. She used to find frogs the size of her thumbnail in her backyard in Florida; sometimes they would cover entire limbs. Once, his lawn mower turned up a nest of baby rattlers.

Finally he remembers the plastic cow. It had a balloon udder you could fill and milk. The teats, bucket and tail (which worked the udder) were white. The rest of the cow was brown.

More and more, the word *guilt* enters his conversation.

Outside, it is getting dark.

Like a marble trapped in a single chute he slides back and forth through the hall between his rooms. Kitchen: milk bottles lined on the floor in one corner, apples and cheese on the table; teapot, strainer, cups and bags, all used, in the sink. Sleeping room: flowers (tulips) in a cup on the desk, returnable bottles stacked like wine bottles (a honeycomb) in the cupboard. Window obscured in a haze of blue lingerie-curtain. On a trunk, two small brass sculptures from a series called *Joy of the Unborn*. They are foetuses entangled in their cords.

As he walks back and forth – pouring beers down the drain, poking at the tea machinery with two fingers – someone traces his steps in the room overhead. Heads and shoulders cant out of windows across the street. Across the street a man stands poking at his belly in the mirror.

Night is falling, filling: he tries various phrases, like strings across his tongue, and abandons them, standing by the window finally, speechless.

The doctor, a woman, Pakistani, arrives and asks what he's on: Meth, pep pills…There are several in her list that he's not heard of. Taking his pulse, she pulls his arm down and glances at the inside of his elbow.

One morning when it is raining a letter arrives. He wonders, Did he know she would write it, Has he been expecting this letter? Her name is typed in the corner, with a brown ribbon.

By the time he gets it back to his room there are spots all over it from the rain, like an unevenly ripe fruit. He props it against the bottle of flowers while he changes clothes, hanging the damp ones on a chair in front of the electric heater. Then he makes tea and sits on the bed to read the letter.

It is badly typed, on blue paper. There are many *x*-ings out; words break off arbitrarily at the right edge of the page and continue a full inch-and-a-half from the left on the line below. This is the first writing of hers he has seen and he looks over the page with interest, thinking how strangely this refutes her general sense of form and order, how easily the typewriter has confounded her.

Her signature is in pencil at the bottom of the second page – a row of bold printed letters, lightly connected–and he quickly turns to see what remains on the last page. It is half-filled with P.S.'s.

1.   The sky is bruised with light.
2.   I have to save us from abstraction.
3.   The knives come out of the mirror like sharks.

Can one's obsessive guilt be cancelled by another's innocence?
He thinks so; he tries.
What qualities does she find common in him and her husband?
A certain shyness, which leads him to such ends as falling off chairs to gain attention; a precise inability to mount stairs; in bed, preoccupation with the cleft between her buttocks; a penchant for leaping through the barriers between rooms.
And he, in her and the other?
The sound of their breath in the dark.
How much has he predicted, to himself?
All but the end. That, like regret, would be against his nature.
Lying here now in the dawn, alone, how does he see the city?
As a thing composed of pale, obscene, gone-off neons. Water trucks sailing slowly down the streets. Milk carts gliding and jangling down the streets. And cats. Cats walk along the sidewalk beside them in utter silence.

My Friend Zarathustra

My friend Zarathustra has stolen my wife.

Yes – I mean what I say, and you must listen; must hear what's not said if you're to understand properly what is said. For, as with him, silence is to me an instinct.

So (I repeat) Zarathustra – carrier of the ashes of the old to the mountains in order to prepare a new beginning, spokesman for the inseparability of creation and destruction, teacher of the eternal recurrence – this same Zarathustra has stolen my wife.

The bastard.

I try to recall, now, when it might have begun between them; at which point, perhaps, she first reached out to touch the hand he offered, but memory fails – I must have been working too hard at the book to take notice. I suppose she may have loved him from the first. That those months of close friendship in the huge house on the hill overgrown with vines – the fires at night as we read together, the fourteen rooms, the quiet, hollow Sundays – concealed all along the slow slide of this fact, and others, beneath me. As I worked in my room on the top floor above the trees. Sometimes when I wake now alone in early morning hours, I imagine there were moments when I felt, dully, never perceiving the truth, that some intangible thing was slipping from me; felt some pale remain of sadness inside, irretrievable. If so, these moments were few, and quickly passed.

(There were times he was happy; he remembers. Now he stands at the window, looking down on the town. Neons are coming on, like exclamation marks for something the darkness is trying to say; they show red on the glass. In the distance radio towers rise against the sky. Fragments accumulate on his desk. He is aware of the space between things. He holds broken facts in his hands.)

Her work grew ever better, the colors bold and the rapid strokes finding relief in sudden, unexpected islands of close detail, ever more explicit, the content increasingly erotic – a body in grey fleshtones with three heads turned each to the others, the lips livid, against a background of alizarins and ochre; my own became increasingly subtle and sparse, moving towards silence. It occurred to none of us, I think, to wonder for so much as a moment whether things outside proceeded along the course which had brought us, or driven us, there; to that sole, solitary refuge.

The hills spread about me now as I write, looking down on the tops of trees. A light fog resides forever inside them. The dampness of it enters the open window of my bedroom each morning, a clean, fresh smell appropriate to new beginnings. The sunrise is splendid, breaking in rainbows through the mist and drifting, light dew; most nights the Northern Lights fan out and fill the sky, as though beautiful cities were burning far away. There is no life anywhere in these trees. Where birds once sang and young deer broke the crust of new-fallen snow.

My work – what can I say of it? I fear I am now past all ambition; that volition, like hope, has died within me and nothing will issue again from that still center. (There would be such comfort in despair.) Times were, a single image, a phrase, would imbue page upon page with life; stories would spring fullblown from the chance word of a friend, the pattern of light through leaves at the window, the eager edge of a razor. Now lifeless pages of notes and scattered scenes accumulate on my table like slices of cheese on a platter: these weak attempts to retrieve my life. This might, I suppose, be expected, a function of the events outside, an equivalent decay.

– Tonight J wants to play for us the piano. He sits on the bench beside her, his face in his hands, weeping. B's fingers form broad X's in the moisture on the tabletop. It is Chopin, she says. The keyboard is roughly sketched out with a carpenter's pencil at one end of the table; there are no halftones. And so we wait.

– This morning we found him in the tub, the drain closed, his own blood all around him; in aspic. His eyes stared up and forward at the tiles on which J has painted a cluster of grapes, and on them, a roach. One of the girls is pregnant. Bits and shreds of half-digested food cling to the sink's sides each morning.

– *Force of circumstances driving the protagonists to the commission of a dreadful act*…

(He is standing at the window. It is open, and he speaks words to it. They scatter on the darkness, random as facts, unforgiving. He has done this before. He will do this again. He is free.)

I remember the last night. We had just made love and she stood at the window, her stomach bulging slightly now and her breasts full, the old stretch-marks lost. The motel sign was red on the glass; darkness entered through the window. And she said, Jim. Jim…we're leaving. When she turned to me, light from the hall glinted on tears in her eyes that, now, would never fall. I'm sorry. After a moment I stood and nodded, then came up here and began to write down everything I remembered about her. At dawn I found I could write no more, and I realized she was gone.

(He is tall, large, with deep blue eyes and heavy ridges above them, like shelves for dark things that might fall out of the sky. He listens to his own voice ringing in the corridors of night. He smiles. It is almost over now.)

It is 3 a.m., a cool night wrapped in clouds, and again unable to sleep, I take down a book. It is a foreign edition and with a small silver knife I must cut the pages free as I read:

We are to recognize how all that comes into being must be ready for a sorrowful end; we are forced to look into the terrors of the individual existence – yet we are not to become rigid with fear: a metaphysical comfort tears us momentarily from the bustle of the changing figures. We are really for a brief moment—

But wait. There are sounds outside now. Voices milling about, feet. Voices. Together.

I go to the window. There are fires. The villagers have come at last.

Free Time

Sometimes I become quite certain that I shall go mad from this preoccupation with women. The rest of me sink in this obsessed mind for good, as in a swamp. I'm passing a shop, a girl is looking into the shop window and I can think of nothing now but her legs and the way her skirt fits over her hips. Want to see her breasts. Will she turn and smile, caught a flash of thigh there, the top of stockings. Walk up the steps. Always so lonely here. And on the trolley devastated, a ruins, all these women I must watch. There doesn't seem to be anything else. Just have them smile for me, feel their skin. Lie by this one, hand on that bare waist. How gentle I would be. Whenever I was going, what I was doing. That doesn't matter now.

I can remember my father. He is coming up the stairs which lead down by stages from our yard here to the street far below. He is carrying something. A paper bag, under his arm. It was taped shut at the store and he has ripped open the side. A flapping, gaping dark gash. He is holding one of the beers in his hand, drinking it as he climbs. Towards me on my first real bicycle.

From my window here I see gulls that have wandered in from the harbor. They drag themselves along above trees, drop to the ground and try to understand what that is. Only once before, in London, have I seen gulls in the middle of a city like this.

At night I lie here listening to country music that comes up from the bar below my room. I've written a song:

> "I just kind of ran out
> Of money and time and friends
> And then I ran out
> On you."

I work during the day, in a department store. At five I sit down with my first martini, away from the windows, and I sing that. Gulls pay no attention, neon signs just go on flashing, traffic does not abate.

You used to meet me downstairs in the street after your Women's Lib meeting. Sometimes I would wait for hours.

I am reworking my destiny with a freedom I said.

But why do you want to make people ashamed of their existence?

I'm sorry. But love is a process like decompression, for the diver.

Like manumission for the slave.

Who is always drowning.

Or already drowned.

And we would walk by the lake.

"If two people love each other there can be no happy end to it."

…Yes you said.

All my friends are killing themselves.

You said: a boy I used to go with read about territorial imperatives. I came home late one night and there he was on my porch pissing on the front door.

Really I said. They are.

With profits from my first book I had companies in all the major cities print thousands of matchbooks with the words "Father where are you?" and my phone number. These were distributed free by diners and truck stops, newsstands, pipe shops, laundromats, sporting goods stores. I got no reply.

_____ has always played a large role in my life. That is to say, whatever I did, it was some memory or occasion of _____ against which I measured it.

Finally, pushed to the wall, I quoted Jung.

As a result of the ego's defective relation to the object – for a will to command is not adaptation – a compensatory relation to the object develops in the unconscious, which makes itself felt in consciousness as an unconditional and irrepressible tie to the object. The more the ego seeks to secure every possible liberty, independence, superiority, and freedom from obligations, the deeper does it fall into the slavery of objective facts. The subject's freedom of mind is chained to an ignominious financial dependence, his unconcernedness of action suffers, now and again, a distressing collapse in the face of public opinion, his moral superiority gets swamped in inferior relationships, and his desire to dominate ends in a pitiful craving to be loved.

I went to see Marc in his hospital room. He hadn't done a very thorough job of it. Some broken bones, low on blood, collapsed lung, colitis. After three one would have thought serious tries. We watched TV on a set that hung from the ceiling.

Leaving the hospital and walking down Portobello Road, I saw a double pram on the pavement outside a shop. One child sat erect with a smile, banging two rattles together. The other had slumped forward on its face. A brightly colored arrow protruded from its back.

My father was not so much absent as irregular: from time to time he would appear with his bags newly covered in customs stamps and claim checks, and those times, for a week, two, a month, he might be with me every waking hour (I seem to recall there were even occasions upon which he came and lay beside me at night); but always would arrive the morning I woke to my mother telling me he was gone, and it then could be a year, or more, before I again saw him.

I have to confess, no, I really must tell you this, that I have no conscience in regard to posterity, absolutely none. For despite the most specific instructions from my translator, and I received a letter just this morning describing exactly what he wished and wished not, indeed would refuse, to see in my future work (I tacked it to the wall above the chair where I work), I go on letting these "stories," these things of mine, have their own way. (As I did, finally, you.)

My next book will be called *The Collected Love Poems of Adolph Hitler*. The one after that, *Krafft-Ebing I Love You*.

One memory of my mother. She is laughing with the rest at my father who is very drunk and men keep bringing her drinks.
I am five, standing by the wall a room away, listening.

Last night I came home from work, set my martini alongside, and copied this into my notebook. From Cocteau:
Sexual vice reflects one of the most intriguing forms of aesthetics.
It is not from taste, as a collector might group furniture and fabrics, that this septuagenarian arranges the smallest details of the scenario without which he cannot satisfy his senses when daylight comes. If he disguises himself as a Louis XV soubrette, if he wears chains and submits to the insults of a telegraphist, and finally opens an obscene telegram signed by his daughter, this occurs after researches and obscure preparations which leave him no choice and

end in a masquerade where his senses desperately construct an equivalent, more baroque, but in fact hardly less individual than any other, for beauty.

My strongest impressions are of my father sitting across the table with a book. I would look at him, his eyes would slide up from the page, he would smile. Then return to the book. One evening as he drank with my mother in the front room, I slipped into the study and examined the stack of books on the table beside his reading chair; I touched each title, mouthing the words to myself. *Traitor Within*, *The Cry for Help*, *Man Against Himself*. *Probleme des Selbstrmordes*. Each volume was a study of suicide.

Bleak Bay

He'd come to Bleak Bay originally because he liked the name. That was in the Sixties, and he'd arrived in the back of an old pickup with a knapsack in his lap. Now it was thirty years later. The knapsack was in a corner of the closet, untouched for years. His wife was in a motel downtown being touched, intimately as they say, by the man she worked for.

This revelation had arrived by phone.

"It's nine o'clock. Do you know where your wife is?" a female voice had said. Minutes later the phone rang again. "If not, you might try the Arlington Motel, room nineteen."

There was no one else it could be, of course, no one but Sanders.

He mixed a drink and sat on the patio listening to crickets fiddle furiously as the night congealed around them. A cat came up the driveway and stood for a moment looking over its shoulder at him before going on.

"Are you asking me out?" she had said when he mumbled something about a movie, then gone off to see to another table. When she came back she said, "I ain't been asked out much – but I've been asked *in* a lot of times. Might even say I've been *taken* in."

"And did you *give* in?" he asked when she next returned.

"A few times." She'd smiled then, sweeping hazel eyes over him quickly. "I get off at nine."

He'd been going there for two weeks, every day twice a day, for breakfast and dinner, since the first time he walked in and saw her. When he picked her up at nine she'd said Forget the movie and taken him to her apartment, an efficiency above a garage just off Main Street. She poured wine into coffee cups, handed him both, and walked out of the kitchen corner into the living room corner, where she fed records into a cabinetlike stereo. Shostakovich's Fifth leapt into the room about them. She turned around and reached for her cup.

"You like this?"

"Oh yes. Almost all Russian music, in fact."

"That's good."

They settled onto the floor near the stereo, backs against the couch that doubled as a bed, and he put his long, skinny arm around her shoulders. She leaned into him.

"Most people 'round here, I put that on and they think it's...I don't know, weird maybe? *Listen* to this: it's like a choir, all that sword-crossing at the first forgotten now, just this peace, this resolve."

They listened together through most of the first movement.

"Where you from, Dave?" she said, face turning towards him.

"East Coast. Near New York."

"Thought so."

"The accent, right?"

"Right. What're you doing down here?"

He shrugged. "Wanted to see what this country was like – all of it, not just my little corner. Hope to write books someday. You a musician?" He gestured towards the stereo.

"Lord no. All I can do to play the radio in tune. But there's something in music like this that's inside me too, all kinds of feelings I can't express. First time I heard this, it was like doors were flying open inside me."

"I felt the same way, but I would never have put it like that."

They kissed then, and the rest of the night followed quickly thereupon. The next day, he and his knapsack moved in for good.

Their son had put himself through school as a programmer and ran his own software company in Hoboken, right across the Hudson from New York.

He mixed another drink, lighter this time. The crickets had quieted; mostly he heard traffic sounds from the interstate. *Wozzeck* unraveled on the turntable just inside patio doors he'd spent a month of weekends installing.

He had never pictured himself settling down, certainly not at nineteen, but there he was, living with her in the efficiency, starting work on the local paper he now edited, listening to music every night. Soon they'd bought a car, then a small house, then a larger one. Days went slowly, years quickly. And over those years they had grown, or been drawn, or fallen, apart, something he failed to realize until the divides were already far advanced. He sat watching death tolls mount in Vietnam and Salvador as she remained, untouched, at the center of her music, her job and friends, their life together in this house. Slowly he rediscovered the world's pain, a pain he had known all too well at nineteen, on the road and open-eyed, and had since forgot.

We are all guilty of everything, Dostoevski said.

Wozzeck ended; the child rode away on his hobbyhorse. Dave rode in his Toyota to the Arlington Motel. At room nineteen he knocked and waited through whispers, bed creaks, footsteps.

"Oh shit," Sanders said.

"Hi, George. I'd like to talk to my wife. I'll wait for her in the coffeeshop."

He ordered coffee for both of them, black for her, cream for him, and after a few minutes she came in and sat beside him at the counter. They drank their coffee and pushed the cups away.

"I'm sorry, Dave."

"I know."

"You need for me to tell you that I didn't mean for this to happen, that I never intended it?"

He shook his head.

"It just started," she said. "This was the first time. Now I guess it's over."

"Are you sorry?"

"A little. Regretful, anyhow."

She looked out the window at passing cars. They were the only customers. The waitress sat at a table drinking iced tea and listening to country music on a portable radio.

"Less and less is possible every year, Dave. You start thinking about all the things you'll never do again."

"Like fall in love?"

"Yes."

He looked at her. "Have you been unhappy, Cathy?"

"No more than most. A lot less than you. I wanted to help you, but I didn't understand. You're not responsible for the world, Dave, you can't be."

"Walk with me?"

He paid and they went out. The moon was full, white as bone. He reached through the open window and pulled out the packed knapsack, swung it over one shoulder.

"I can't say that I'll be back, or that I won't be. Maybe by the time I can, it won't matter to you. I took a little money, a couple hundred, and some clothes. Everything else is yours." He watched tears gather in hazel eyes. How can we be so full of memories, so strangely fulfilled, at these times? "Be happy, Cathy."

Half a mile down the road she pulled up beside him in the car.

"Give you a lift as far as the highway?" she said.

He got in.

Alaska

Julie McCargar, the charge nurse most days on 7-3, walked past me down the hall shaking her head.

"They keep on rolling bodies in," she said. It was something she said a lot.

Morning had been a bitch by any standards, beginning with Pam catching twins that shot out like bubbles from a frog's mouth as she stood by a gurney in the chaos desperately trying to get report from dog-tired Wayne at a quarter to seven, continuing soon after with a traffic pile-up that brought in two Care Flite choppers, four or five ground units and close to forty family members who arrived from home partially dressed, eyes lit with terror, and stood cluttering up the ER's mouth till we finally had security and the ER cop clear them out. Now it was early afternoon and things had let up. Every floor and cabinet top was heaped with detritus: ripped-out IV bags, sterile wrappers for bandages and clamps and tubes, plastic syringes, trays and basins scattered about and themselves overflowing.

"For God's sake let's try to pull it together before the next wave comes in," Julie was saying as I walked into the nurse's station near the front of the unit. Through glass partitions we could see a waiting room as trashed out in its own way as the trauma and treatment rooms, but less than a dozen patients now waited in the mauve and lime-green plastic chairs. Julie turned to me. "Laura could probably use some help in meds-4, Tony. They've been on a holding pattern in there for a while now." Then she went out the chute fast, pursuing an intern who'd just walked by.

Meds-4 was at the far end of the hall, a converted storage space used chiefly for holding triaged patients till we could get around to them, minor accidents and the like.

Laura was leaning against the wall and writing on chart sheets splayed out over the counter. Seated on a chair with her back to me, hunched about herself the way people with central pain do, was a woman with shortish blond hair cut to the same length all around. Her head was down, the back of her neck a smooth, separate plane. Over the chair's back I could see on her black T-shirt three letters of an arc, E-T-A, and part of a fourth, an O, or possibly a G, with what I took to be a disembodied eye floating above them.

Laura looked up and said in a whisper: "Come in very slowly."

The woman held a large bird cradled in her arms with her face down close to it. Her eyes swiveled up to me as I came to her side, then, in surprise, she made to straighten her head and look full on but winced and cried out.

"Hello, Susan."

"You two know one another?" Laura said.

I nodded and walked around in front. The bird, a hawk I now saw, and a young one, had one talon through Susan's right cheek. There was a runnel of blood down it, and when she opened her mouth I could see the rest of the talon moving about inside.

"It hurts like a sonofabitch, Tony."

"We've got the bird sedated," Laura said. "And the vet from the zoo sent along a note. This should have been seen a long time ago." She waved sketchily towards the hall. "You know. Dr. Talbott's on his way back down from O.R. now."

"Tony…"

"Don't try to talk, Suze." Then to Laura: "What happened?"

"Miss Gomez works as an assistant at the zoo. She was taking the bird out of its cage for a feeding when something – they think probably a copter that flew over just then – made it panic. It tried to fly, and before Miss Gomez could get a better hold –"

"The hawk did."

"Right," Laura said, and went back to her charting.

"I didn't know you were back in town," I told Susan. "Wait a minute. Here." I handed her a pad of old order sheets chopped into rough quarters and stapled across the top for use as scratch paper. It was a sickly, pale green and would end up as shopping lists, phone numbers, crib sheets for vital signs, resuscitation records. I took a pen out from among the scissors, hemostats and penlights of my labcoat pocket and gave that to her as well.

Keeping one arm cradled under the hawk, she balanced the pad on her thigh and wrote with the other hand, barely touching paper with pen, it seemed, tiny letters in handwriting that had in it something of the roll and flow of her parents' language with all those terminal, run-on O's and A's.

Never left.

"But your letter…"

Only way I could do it. Couldn't see you.

"It was terrible for a long time without you, and impossible. Then it was only terrible."

And?

"Then I guess it was over."

She wrote something quickly, scratched it out, looked up at me out of the corners of her eyes. They were turquoise, sometimes blue, often green, with large pupils almost filling the iris and in strong light leaving only a rim of color that made one think of eclipses.

Me too.

Together we had been a small Alaska, our own six-month white night. Sleep was a strange bedfellow to us both. Susan went to sleep instantly then woke an hour or two later to pass the night prowling about the apartment and returning perfunctorily, again and again, to bed, where covers eddied up about her. Then the drinking would start. I could never fall asleep and lay there heavily conscious of her arm across my chest, of her presence in another room or breath on my shoulder, at last sinking towards semi-consciousness at three or four in the morning when she had abandoned all pretense to sleep. I would open weighted eyes to her profile against the white wall and watch as memory, night thoughts, a peculiar softness I came to know well, washed over her features.

In the hallway a prisoner from county jail walked by with a deputy alongside. He wore cuffs with a long chain, and blood ribboned down his chest from multiple cuts on neck and shoulders. A faded tattoo moved jerkily like an early cartoon character on his upper arm when he flexed the muscle there. His skin, possibly from tanning agents, was an unnatural yellowish-brown.

Neal Talbott came in, nodded to Laura and me, and knelt by Susan's chair. He moved his upper body around, looking at things from several angles, occasionally probing gently with one finger at her cheek. Talbott is from British working-class stock, with little taste or place in his life for the esoteric. Everything about him says that even the most complex tasks are accomplished in a series of practical, small maneuvers.

He half-turned, still on one knee, and told Laura what he would need: Novocaine and Valium drawn up, dressing tray, fine and gross suture kits, Betadine scrub, size seven gloves.

Then to Susan: "You'll be a solo act again in just a few moments, dear. There'll be only a small scar which should pretty much fade within a month or two. But just to be sure, we'll have Plastics take a look."

I've always envied people like Neal Talbott, for whom obstacles and impediments are not so much easily overcome as unacknowledged in the first place. They skate through life on solid ice, warmly wrapped, mind and eye focused, invigorated by the exercise. Our minds are printed circuits, I think, snapped into place at birth, and we can't do a lot about the way those circuits fire.

He draped Susan with a sheet and scrubbed the area around the wound, moving slowly so as not to frighten the bird. Instinctively he held his head close to it, humming tunelessly as he worked.

Laura had pulled over a rolling tray and stood by it handing him 4x4's, bottles of Betadine, swabs, alcohol. A smaller tray held suture kits, sterile wrappings torn back and hanging down over the side of the tray like a skirt. Susan had her eyes squeezed shut, and I could see muscles jumping in her jaw as she ground her back teeth. I went over and took her free hand in mine. It fit the way it always had.

Neal injected Novocaine subcutaneously both inside and outside Susan's cheek, gave it time to catch hold, then flicked a scalpel briefly above and below the talon, opening a slit like an episiotomy, less than a centimeter on each side, talking alternately to the hawk and to Susan in low tones.

"This is the tricky part," he said.

Leaning in close to the bird, he put thumb and finger inside Susan's mouth and grasped the hawk's talon. Then he gently took hold of the part just outside and began to ease it through the opening, pulling the digit straight. I caught a glimpse of his finger outside Susan's cheek then – and it was done.

The hawk immediately retracted its foot, pulling it in close to its body, but made no further move. Susan sat up straight, arching her back. You could feel tension falling off walls and ceiling. I squeezed Susan's hand and let go.

"We have a launch," Neal said, and started prepping for sutures.

He used finest silk and set the sutures close together in a precise row. It looked, when he had finished, like the spine of some intricately small and delicate animal.

"I'll have Plastics nip down for a look," Neal said as he washed up at the sink, "but I do believe we're home free." He came over and put a hand briefly on Susan's shoulder. Then to Laura: "Anybody know what we're supposed to do with the bird?"

"I'll take it back with me," Susan said. "Thank you."

"Nothing," Neal said, and was gone, swinging out into the hall with his labcoat waving in the wake, on to new solutions. Julie came in to tell Laura she was needed in trauma-1 for a full arrest four minutes out if things were wrapped up here. I wet a washcloth for Susan, handed it to her along with a towel, and started cleaning up the room.

"You left the paper?"

I nodded. "One too many obits. Two too many society fundraisers."

"How long have you been here?"

"Almost a year now."

She wiped her face vigorously everywhere else, gently around the tiny spine there on her cheek. Mascara had smeared below her eyes, giving her a vaguely clownlike look. Her cheek was faintly gold from the Betadine. An X-ray machine lumbered past in the hall, nosing chairs and trashcans from its path.

"I don't drink anymore," she said, and when I turned to answer, she had pulled up her skirt, opened her legs. It could have been accidental, I suppose, and she went on pulling clothes back into order. For a moment I felt as one does upon coming into the curve towards home at the end of a long, exhausting trip.

"That's wonderful," I said.

"Well..." She stood, still cradling the hawk, one hand pressed down on its feet, fingers intertwined with them. "I'd better be getting back. Hate to lose this job. It's the only good one I've ever had."

"What about Plastics?"

She shrugged. "You have a phone these days?"

I shook my head.

She touched my cheek, lightly, and when she did, the hawk rustled its wings, causing her to take her hand away.

"You're a good man, Tony," she said.

I tossed the last patches of gauze, a handful of disposable forceps, scalpels, tweezers and tiny needles curved like scimitars, into trash and Sharps containers. Everything in life seems to happen either very slowly or very fast. Things from which we will not recover, heart attack, huge trucks, Alaskas, are bearing down on us, careening into our lives.

Upstairs in ICU are the ones we almost saved. Their hearts go on, and they breathe, and that is all they do. For a moment, standing at the threshold, I hear their call, a sound like whale songs slipping through cracks from a world we cannot imagine, settling on me from the limitless blue above.

Kazoo

Walking down the street on my way to see The Leech, I'm attacked by this guy who jumps out of the alley shouting *Hai! Hai! Feefifofum!* (you know: bloodcurdling) over and over, cutting air with the sides of his hands. He says *Hai!* again, then *Watch out, man! I'm gonna lay you open!* He's still assaulting the air, battering it too.

My, I think, *an alley cat.* Then I stand off and kind of watch this little dance he's doing. Dispassionately in front, you see, but I get to admiring it. I mean, he's cutting some great steps, beating hell out of the air. I snap my fingers for him, clap a little.

You watch out, man! he says. *You get cute, I'm gonna hurt you bad, put you through that wall there.* Then he goes back to his *Hai!* and *Feefifofum!* He's standing off about three yards from me, jumping around, chopping his hands back and forth, looking mean, a real hardankle. He's about five foot and looks like he might have modeled for Dylan Thomas' bit about the "bunched monkey coming."

By this time there's quite a crowd piling up. They're all standing around clapping, snapping their fingers, digging the action. Some guy in like black heads in to sell *Watchtowers* and this Morton pops up and starts passing around stone tablets and pillows of salt. There's a spade out on the edge of the crowd, he's picking pockets, got three arms. Deep Fat Friar passes by, frowns, goes on down the street flogging himself with a vinyl flyswatter. And there's this cop on the fringe giving out with a mantra of dispersal. *Ibishuma, go go; Ibishuma, go go* (don't think he had it quite right, you know?).

One guy pulls out a set of plastic spoons and commences to make them go clackety-clack, clackety-clack between his thumb and great toe. Another guy has a kazoo. Someone else is trying to get them to do Melancholy Baby. *Take your clothes off and be adancin' bare*, this smartass yells out of the back of the crowd. He *is* kinda hairy, this guy.

Come on, Ralph, he shouts at me. *Come on, man, we're gonna tangle. Hai! Feefifofum!* But you can tell he likes it, the attention I mean, because he goes up on his toes and pirouettes.

I stand there looking at him, frowning a little, dispassionate again. I mean, I'm getting kind of tired of the bit by now. Some guy comes by about then with a monkey on his back, grinding at a nutchopper. Another one's hunkered-down on the corner to demonstrate his Vegamatic; his buddy's scraping bananas. And there's this like arthritic wobbling down the sidewalk with a Dixie cup, begging green-stamps.

Hai! Hai! Hing! (That last one way up in the nose.)

He stops and drops his hands, looks down at the concrete, shuffles his feet. *Aw come on Ralph*...Then he's *Hai!*-ing and *Feefifofum!*-ing again, going at it like mad, jumping around like a spastic toad.

And by this time I'm beginning to get *real* tired. I mean, I put up with his bag through here but now I'm gonna be late to see The Leech, so I – and let this be a lesson to all of you–I move in for the kill. I've been watching Captain Conqueroo on the morning tube, you see, and I'm like eager to try this thing out. So when this guy sees me coming and charges in like a rhinoceros or something, I just step ever so casually to one side and with a sudden blur of motion I get him with the Triple-Reverse Elbow Block, lay it right on him. He folds up like a letter that's getting put in an envelope that's too small for it and he falls down in slow motion. His tongue's hanging out and a fly's walking up it toward his teeth.

Name's not Ralph, I tell him. Then I stand there humming along with the spoons and kazoo till he can breathe again. Which doesn't take him over twenty minutes or so – we'd only got through Black Snake Rag, Mountain Morning Moan and part of America the Beautiful (raga form).

Anyhow, he starts coming back from violet toward the pinkish end of the spectrum, and he looks up at me and he says, *Aw gee, Algernon. Look, give me a chance. Sorry I bugged you.* Saying that reminds him of something and he stops long enough to spit out the fly. *Wasn't my idea*, he goes on. *Nothing personal against you, guy told me to do it…Bartholomew?*

I shake my head. I kick him a little. *Who.*

Guy just came up to me at the bus stop, told me you were on your way to the bank, don't know who he was. Said if I beat you up I could have the money and if I didn't he'd send his parakeet out to get me…Chauncey?

I kick him again. *Big guy? Southerner? Hair looked like a helmet? Scar where his nose should be, cigar stuck in it?*

Yeah…Look, you wouldn't be Rumplestiltskin by any chance?

Sorry. I tell him that as I'm kicking him.

Didn't think so.

I reach down to help him up, since he's obviously going to need help. *That'd be Savannah Rolla, a friend of mine*, I tell him. Savvy's a film-maker and I know he and a poet-type by the name of Round John Virgin are hassling with a love epic called *Bloodpies* – in which the symbols of the mudcake, the blood bath, the cow patty and innocent youth find their existential union – so I look around for the cameras. But I can't spot them.

I'm on my way to the blood bank, I tell the guy. He's got a funny sense of humor, Savannah does. Do anything for a friend, though. And since his hand's in mine anyway since I'm helping him up, I shake it.

Ferdinand Turnip, I introduce myself. *Ferdinand. My wife is a Bella, name's Donna.*

Percival Potato, he says, and gives me this big grin like he's busting open. *Mad to greet you.* He's giving me the eye, so I take it and put it in my wallet right next to the finger someone gave me the day before.

We talk a while, have lunch together in the laundromat, then it's time for me to split. We notice the band's still going at it and Percy cops a garbage can and heads over to blow some congadrum with them. I walk a mile, catch a camel, and rush to the blood bank. I realize I've left all my beaver pelts at home again, so I take off one of my socks (the red one) and give it to the driver. He blows his nose on it, thanks me, and puts it in his lapel.

At the blood bank Dr. Acid, who's the head, tells me The Leech is dead from overeating. Dr. Acid has three friends: Grass, who's rooting around in the drawers; Roach, who looks like a leftover; and Big H, who rides a horse – Joint has the bends and is taking the day off. They're all eating popcorn balls and scraping bits of The Leech off the wall, putting the pieces in a picnic basket that has a place for bottles of wine too. They ask me to stay for a potluck dinner, but I say no. I cop some old commercials with them for a while, then I dive out of the window and swim to my studio. Someone's dumped Jello in the water, and it's pretty tough going. The crocs are up tight today, but the piranha seem placid enough.

At the studio, reverently, I apply the 65th coat to my *Soft Thing* – four more to go. I got the idea from Roy Biv, a friend of mine. Each layer of paint is a step up the spectrum, a solid color. I have carefully calculated the weight of my paint, canvas, medium. The last brush stroke of the 69th coat, and my painting will fall through the floor. It will be a masterpiece of aesthetic subtlety.

By the time I've drunk all the turpentine and finished burning the brushes, it's willy-nilly time to dine. But the lemmings are bad in the hall so I'm late catching my swan and I have to wait on top of the TV antenna for over an hour. Then by the time I get home, the vampires are out. They wave as I pass. Everyone knows you can't get blood from a Turnip – and anyway, they're all saps.

I go in and Donna comes up and kisses me and puts her arm around me and tells me she doesn't love me anymore. I look out the window. Sure enough, the world's stopped going 'round.

So I go in the john and find my kazoo and I play for a long time.

Bubbles

D—,where are you now?

I've searched for you down in the cove, by the little sandstone temple that the Greek built when his daughter married, where a wild cat lives, all butter and ginger; in the Soho pubs and Hampstead house parties; down by the docks where the air smells of banana, oil floats out on the water (Ophelia's gowns), and spiders crept across the top of my black shoes that stood like open graves on the whitewashed boards.

Once, I asked after you at the small café on the bridge by Paddington Station and a man in the corner, overhearing, paused with a forkful of soft dry cheese in front of his mouth (his forefinger nicotine-stained halfway down between the joints) and spoke across the room through already-parted lips: "Kilroy, you say? Ah yes, he was here. Remember him well; almost like my own son, he was. Yes, he was here" – then delivered the fork and chewed: a mouthful of crumbling custard. On the brown table beside him sat his teeth, poundnotes clenched between them, a pink moneyclip in the morning sun.

("Love, hate indifference," you used to say in your flamboyant way, "they can work wonders, miracle. If you have belief." And – flamboyantly, extravagantly–I believed. In you. And now have only this, all this guilt, that bangs away inside me.)

Outside the café now, four men point in four directions and step backwards until they come together. A delivery boy in white pedals along the bridge and stops before me, returning undelivered another of the cables by which I have tried to reach you:

> Yesterday the cows came
> home stop Bailey expected
> later today stop Where
> are you stop

On the opposite wall of the bridge someone has spraypainted *Kilroy the saviour*. "Is it true, sir?" the delivery boy asks. "Can he really do all they say he can?" I go over and scrape the white letters off into an envelope, marking it *near Paddington Station, 4 Jan, 6 AM*. Does this mean he has left the city? A lorry comes by, killing the delivery boy, who has tried to follow me across the street.

And so I go walking down Westbourne Grove where teddy bears hang by their ears on clotheslines, where marzipan elephants lounge in the palms of children and American Indians camp in the dustbins, their salty teepee smoke spiraling up between the Queen Anne houses. Leaning against one of the spear fences, a flophatted old man blows his nose into a tiny rag of flannel then holds it out away from his eyes, looking to see what he's brought up, like a fisher, from the deeps. "Hey, got a sixpence?" – and his huge nostrils hang there in front of my face like two black holes in the morning. As always, walking – its regularity, the rhythm of it – brings me to another kind of rhythm; I always end up singing or, in busier parts of the city, humming quietly to myself. So now as I walk (hopefully towards you) over the gobbets of paint and the heelspores of crushed orange chalk, past the walls and fences painted with six-foot flowers and diminutive Chinese dragons, past the bakeshops with their pastel façades, I'm singing softly to myself *Jesus wants me for a sunbeam*.

Who would have thought it. When we squatted together in piles of dust behind the books upstairs, sharing the last disposable yellow paper robe (luckily a 44, so it fitted us perfectly) and nibbling at the cake of vanilla seaweed we found in a drawer when we took the flat? That you should leave, and months later the realization of what had happened would come so suddenly upon me, and with such force, that I would sit for days without moving or speaking, until friends came at last and carried me away. That finally, obsessed with the depth of my guilt and loss, I should come searching for you, asking everywhere, sending these messages out ahead of me (cables, phonecalls, bits of paper thrown out the window to passers-by), out from my tiny room in Clapham Common, and following these signs across all of London: chalk on brick walls, letters sprayed from cans, empty chocolate wrappers which could be yours ...

On the street in front of a fish shop two children are killing one another with wooden swords while all the silver-bubble fisheyes watch them calmly and dogs sit across the street quietly looking on. Farther down, where wind has rattled windows, a burglar alarm clangs. In this amazing new stillness a young man enters a nearby dentist's office ("Half a pint, sir? Three bob, please; just put this over your face") and emerges giggling. The window is filled with old dental tools toppling in lines off the velvet-covered shelves and looking like instruments for exquisite torture: the relics of orbicular inquisitions.

In Notting Hill Gate (I wonder if you remember this) the buildings catch the wind and lay it like a ribbon down along the pavement; it swirls about my ankles, clinging, resilient, as I tramp through. Three one-man bands glare at one another from the corners of an intersection, waiting for the light. The flowerseller's black Alsatian is wearing a chain of daisies at its neck; it can catch pennies on its tongue. Remembering the old man's nostrils on Westbourne Grove, I make for the tube station – then bump bump bump (down the funny stairs from the tipitittitop). One wall is covered with telephone numbers; vast 69's scratched into the cement with belt-buckles or penknives; a poem in red shoe polish:

>During the raids
>the lost plane
>reported
>the war over
>the pilot missing

On the other, in a tiny elegant script, is penciled: *When Kilroy returns.* I stop and with people staring over my shoulder scrape the minute gray flakes off into an envelope.

The third level is deserted. I stand alone by the track, hearing the far-off rumble of trains and the dim, flat voices that float after me, tangling together, down the corridors behind. I turn to look down the rails and when I turn back, a cleaning machine is rushing towards me, its tiny mechanical arm erect out in front like a bull's horn. Quickly I step back against the wall, into the leering two-dimensional arms of a Chinese prostitute. *"Look out! Mind!"* the little machine shouts — penny-sized speaker rattling, distorting under the load — then pulls to a stop just past me and comes slowly backwards.

"Who," it asks (the arm quivering), "are you" (arm stabbing out towards me). "I" (bending back on itself to point, dead center, at itself from above) "am The Machine. *Look out for The Machine!*" A pause. "I'll get you, you know; going to take your place, replace you, do away with your sort." (The arm stabs out again, almost to my knee.) "And about time, too. *So look out!* I'm giving you fair warning now!"

It starts away; then stops, purrs a moment and returns, the little treads lugging sadly backwards.

"What are you doing here!" it demands. "Let me see your passport! Would you like your shoes shined. They need it. I have some nice red polish."

I back away from the arm.

"Kilroy," I say quickly. "Have you seen him; has he been here?"

"Kilroy! You know Kilroy! Yes, he was here!" The little machine pauses, waving its arm thoughtfully. "*He* listened to me. We used to sit here for hours, talking over philosophical problems — mostly ethics, I remember. That was before he went away." The arm droops. "A good man. Sometimes, thinking about a man like that, it almost makes me want to forgive you for everything. Almost." The arm suddenly springs back to life, full of excitement. "Do you know where he is!"

"I'm afraid not. I'm trying to find him."

The arm wilts again. "The only one who ever had enough sense, enough compassion, to listen. He knew I was right..."

"When I do, I'll let you know, and tell him that you asked after him." I turn and start back up the corridors, but the little machine shoots around in front of me.

"Just a moment," it says. "I'm supposed to give you a riddle, you know, before I can let you go." It sits for several minutes, the tiny arm flopping and waving, in deep thought. "But I can't think of one just now. Would you like to hear me clap my hand. I suppose it's all right for you to pass, since you know Kilroy. But I should have something done about those shoes if I were you."

I walk up the tunnel. Behind me the little cleaners shouts: "You don't have much time left, you know. *Watch out for The Machines!*" — and goes zooming away down the concrete beside the tracks. The last syllable had blurred, rattling like a cough; apparently the speaker had finally been too much strained, and the diaphragm had cracked.

I climb back up past all the posters of women in yellow swimwear and the ticket machines into the crowds. It's five now, and the streets are full of dogs. As I walk past a row of phone booths outside a Wimpy Bar, one of the phones rings. I beat the others there and pick it up:

"Yes?"

"We've found him." Outside, it's raining; this booth contains me perfectly, with the water breaking on the gray glass, destroying the world outside.

"Where?"

"There's been an accident. Mercy Hospital. He's asking for you. Hurry." The rain is washing cigarette butts up under the door and into the booth. On a minicab sign someone has written on the cab's window: *He slept here.* Not bothering this time to collect the message, I ring for a cab.

At the hospital I'm greeted by a nurse in layers of diaphanous white that slide over one another, with pink somewhere underneath. She's painted black rims around her eyes, and has a pink-white mouth.

"This way, hurry. He's been asking for you. It may be all that's keeping him alive, making him hold on."

We go down white tile halls where everyone else walks near the walls; the center is new and clean. Then into a room full of soft murmurs and liquid sounds. Five surgeons squat in one corner talking together quietly. A nurse kneels by the bedside crying. Outside the window four young girls stand still and straight, and sing.

He lies on the bed under a clear plastic tent, with the sheets pulled up to his chin. All around him the air is filled with tubes and small, pumping engines. Fluids run bubbling through the tubes; go slowly down, and more quickly up, along them. It's as though his blood system, lymph system – all the delicate soft machinery of his body – have been brought out into the world, redirected through glass and plastic. He is larger than the rest of us. (I remember the long months I lay still and dazed, recovering from the loss of your leaving. Perhaps it was here that I lay. My guilt sustains me.)

When the nurse folds back a flap in the tent he opens his eyes, and I hear the soughing of the pumps more distinctly.

"You...came." When he speaks, the fluids run faster in the tubes, gurgling in time with his voice. Bubbles forming, bursting, passing slowly, like fisheyes, along the tubes.

"I...told them...you would." His eyes are gray, pupil and iris barely distinguishable from the rest. It occurs to me now that he can see nothing; I could be anyone; it wouldn't matter. (And how you smiled and brought coffee and talked to me quietly. Your face was always so different, so changed, in the dark.)

"I...knew you...would." There is a gentle hissing as the nurse opens the oxygen valve a degree wider. (The way I stood at the window, watching, not yet understanding. Afterwards, the room seemed...larger. I was aware of the space between things.)

"Bless...you."

Fluids jumped in the tube (*bubble bubble bubble:* the rhythm of a laugh) and now are still, as the pumps shut off. There is only the hiss of oxygen coming into the tent, out into the room. One huge bubble hangs motionless at the bend of a tube, watching.

"Is he dead?"

The nurse goes over to speak with the doctors. They listen carefully, tilting their heads towards her, and nod. The nurse returns:

"Yes."

So I go into the hall and stand there looking out at the polished green grass and flowers in the hospital lawn. A vine which has climbed the building is now blossoming, scattering leaves down into the yard. It looks like the veins in a hand. Flowers climb along it towards the roofs.

"I'm sorry..." She comes up behind me.

"You needn't be. It wasn't him."

"Then who? Your guilt –"

"I don't know." I turn to face her. The pink-white lipstick is smudged at one corner of her mouth. Should I tell her? How much she resembles his wife; that this may have made it easier for him, near the end? "I don't know who he was. I've never seen him before." I start down the hall and she comes after me.

"Please. Just a moment. This." She holds out a large manila envelope: bulky, jangling. "His personal effects, what he had in his pockets. I wonder...could you take them? Please." I take the envelope from her and leave. Hardly anyone in the halls now. The sun is slanting in through the window, moving out across the tiles. When I turn my head to look back at the vine, it almost blinds me. But the flowers are spilling up over the edge of the roof.

Later, on the street, I open the envelope and spread the things out on top of a low wall. It contains: thirty-nine ha'pennies, two sixpences marked EM in red ink, a child's gyroscope top, and a number of small white envelopes containing bits of paint and graphite, each with a place and date scrawled on the outside.

Farther along the wall in black chalk: *We shall be reborn.* Conceivably. But I've used all my envelopes. The only unsealed one I have is the one with the dead man's things – so I scrape the chalk off into that and mark it *Mercy.* (Tomorrow I will have to return to the phonebooth.) And go walking softly down the street towards home. With a song in my mouth.

Like eyelids, all the windows are open, rolled up on their cords. And night blooms over the heads of the buildings.

Saguaro Arms

Because the jaguars have no spots, at first we don't see them in the room's corners. Shadows, perhaps: nothing more. Though we hear the sound of their breathing from acoustic niches formed in those moments the radio falls silent.

Earlier we listened to NPR, the same news as that we left behind, as though, thrown across our backs or tucked into the corners of boxes and trunks, we have brought these events along with us. Reports on escalating violence, on the collapse of yet another cease-fire and subsequent forfeiture of this week's "safe zone" in San Marco's revolution. Grown large on hunger and despite, now the children of the original freedom fighters are coming down from the hills.

How terrible, Carey says as I open a second bottle of wine, a Brazilian cabernet, auguring down into the cork, working the machine's arms (shaped like a woman's legs) to lever out the cork with a satisfyingly plosive exclamation, and refill our glasses. How sad.

Yes, I say. Life.

But how can we accept it.

Life?

No, the terribleness of it. The sadness.

As though we could do anything else – but I do not say this.

Outside, blackbirds flush from power lines, sweep away in a flat arc and, clustering, drawn to some unseen center, return. They settle back at random on the lines, like musical notes, perforations on player-piano rolls, braille.

What kind of life can they have had, after all, Carey asks.

Or any of us – another thing I don't say. As this lowering sun hauls down its carry-on luggage of remorse.

I stand looking at the bottle's label, a Brazil shape formed of grapes. It resembles Texas, which we have crossed on the way here.

Carey wears the cranberry-color shirt that brought us together, a consoling gift from mother Jeanne. Carey's latest relationship had crumbled to disinterest and disaffection, while my own year-long romance stammered and tripped and blathered away, trying to explain itself, like a poor comedian. Great shirt, I said. She told me about it. We went for coffee. Bare bones of narrative.

Nights when she wears it Carey washes the shirt by hand and puts it out to dry on a hanger over the tub. *Calais. Made in U.S.A.* Seated on the toilet, I keep watch. One corner of the front pocket is stained with ink. The narrow seam along the bottom has begun unraveling. Threads like a plant's tendrils reach down for the tub.

And so, ponderously, as though on camelback, swaying, over desert and between dunes, we've come to this foreign land, where the sun fights its way down through layers of color, where saguaro lift arms in welcome all around us and salamanders with cowlike skulls sail the backs of lit windows each night.

And where, too, rising from the couch beside me from which we've watched "authentic" recreations of live, unrecorded broadcasts of Armstrong Circle Theater, Playhouse 90 and Dave Garroway, you go off to sleep alone in the nest of blankets and pillows you've made of our bathtub.

There, in that other country, my name is remembered. Here I work at whatever I can find.

You think of the child at these times, I know, smallest of the things we left behind. Newborn, with perfect tiny fingernails at the end of plump fingers, the child would not look at us however we hailed and drew it. Picked up, it went rigid. Turned right or left in its crib, it remained there till the whole weight of its skull settled to that side.

We had barely ensconced ourselves here when the jaguars appeared. At first we ignored them. During the journey, after all, there had been so many dangers. Nor are the dangers necessarily over, I feel. Each morning elderly men in crewcuts and bolo ties emerge from behind the redundant locks of ranchstyles to run up the flag. Each evening they emerge again to retrieve those flags. All day they stand peering out their windows, light from massive TV's washing up behind them like a tide. These men bear watching.

As you settle into your tub then, night closing around you, day hanging out backstage bitching with the other bit players till it's time to go on, I sit listening to neighborhood gunfire, to the wheeze and pump of accordions through Juan's window next door.

From their corners the jaguars watch me. Even after I turn off the lights their eyes gleam and flicker. Against moonlight on the back of my windows, as on photographic plates, appear the silhouettes of salamanders, perhaps a dozen of them, facing this way and that. Like myself, like the jaguars, awaiting what I will do next.

Three Stories

Afterwards

You were still alive then, and it was harder. It's not easy now, but I know the memories I have are all I *will* have.

I'd moved into a new apartment and, mornings, stood looking into the mirror over the rim of my tea cup, wondering if my sad eyes (you always called them that) had grown sadder. I ran in a nearby park twice a day, filled the other hours as best I could. I walked a lot. There wasn't much room in my head for anything but you and trying to understand why you were gone.

I still don't know if that last time was a mistake, if things might not have been better except for that. I play it over and over in my head, the way I replay so much of our life together, and I can never decide. It's all such a meld of good things and bad.

You'd been gone three weeks, and called to say you'd like to see me that Monday, that we had a lot to talk over. I picked you up at 12:30. Within the hour we were in bed at the old apartment, sun pushing in through blinds, hubbub of quarrels and children all about us.

Afterwards you dozed and, waking, rolled against me, the warmth of your skin, its weight, so familiar. Country music on the radio: your music.

"I really did want to kill myself," you said. "When I woke up still alive, I was furious."

"But why?" I said after a time.

"Don't ask hard questions." You rolled away for a pull of beer, Molson's Golden, and came back. Your hand lay on my leg like a promise. "One time in ICU, when I was on the ventilator, I came to briefly and someone was rubbing me between the legs." You took your hand away. "Like this," you said as I watched. We made love again then, and you slept. I got up for a beer and sat watching. For most of our last month together, after you came back from the hospital, you had slept. I sat for hours watching the long slope of your back, your unguarded breast, half-closed eyes. So many memories crowded into my mind. I felt so much for you then, such tenderness and sorrow.

In the car going back you told me that you couldn't go on hurting me and thought it would be easier this way. I watched you in yellow top and shorts walk away from me, the last time I saw you.

There was so much I should have said, so much I wanted to say. Some of it, a little, I put in the letters; one day I wrote you eight of them. Some of it I can never say, because it's unsayable. All the important things are, Wittgenstein tells us.

This was months ago, of course.

Gradually it became my apartment, this shell I'd moved into. I set routines that got me through the day. I sat in bars and restaurants and talked to strangers. I settled into work on a new book, one I'd begun when we were first together, sitting at the window downstairs and writing a page or so as you soaked in your bath, putting it away when you came back down to join me.

This morning at four I finished the book, drank half a bottle of gin, and slept. Around eleven I was heading towards the park to run when the apartment manager came to the office door and called out. I have a message for you, she said, handing me a small slip of yellow paper. I'm sorry, she said. She closed the door.

The paper told me you had died that morning in the emergency room at John Peter Smith. I still don't know who called.

I tucked the paper into my shorts, walked on to the park, and ran – ran with tears rolling on my face, sweat pouring from my body. When I got back, the ink had bled off the paper and there wasn't anything left of you. The apartment was small, and mine. I had a life, also small now, to go on with, whatever didn't happen in it.

Running Away

At the police station downtown the restroom on the third floor is locked because drunks and the homeless come in off the streets at night and sleep there. The officer who gives him the key tells him this with a smug assumption of accord. The building is old and shabby, with paint flaking from every wall, stairs worn dangerously swayback, great automobile-like dents in the filing cabinets.

Returning the key to the desk he sees her in a small room just beyond, sitting behind another girl who stares out into the squadroom drooling onto her AC/DC T-shirt. She, the runaway, is looking at the wall; her shoulders are hunched.

It's two o'clock in the morning and they've come to retrieve a daughter. Grounded for two weeks, she left a dramatic note and ran away. It was a scale-model runaway, to the dimensions of her life: six blocks to the mall and a phone call to a friend whose mother picked her up. There she was found by police, handcuffed and brought downtown. With her are the girl who drools and stares with doll's eyes, an 11-year-old prostitute, another runaway, a teenager who attacked her teacher with a razor.

The mother is hysterical and self-accusing, the father withdrawn. Institutions like this are nothing new to him, nor are the streets; he has survived both; he wants this only to be over. They answer questions, sign documents. The officer who picked her up talks to them for a moment and says they have a nice girl there, he hopes this will help them get things straightened out and if there's anything he can do to help just let him know. The girl is brought out. She does not look at them. She is told to check the contents of her purse and sign a release. An officer has a few final words with her. She says nothing.

They all walk, together for the last time, outside. Street-cleaning trucks are about, lobbing great tides of water onto the sidewalk and curbs. He watches the water break around his shoes. He unlocks and holds the door for each of them, starts the car, turns on the radio: Bartok. "Not *that* stuff again," his daughter says. He turns it off. The jagged city landscape heaves up over the car's hood as he tries to find his way through a labyrinth of one-way streets that keep delivering them back to the central city. He passes one newsstand four times. Then at last finds access to an interstate heading south.

In the backseat their daughter falls asleep. His wife looks steadily ahead into oncoming lights. He turns the radio on low, something large, shapeless, romantic. They pass the state hospital, a mile-long junkyard, the airport, and turn onto the narrow road that will take them home. Stores at roadside, closed many hours ago, are brightly lit. There is little traffic.

He is thinking about the time he sent flowers to her at the office, roses, simply because she'd told him she had always hoped someone might do that someday. Friends, she said years later, had told her that she just *had* to hold on to him. One morning, turning to him in bed, she said that all she'd ever wanted was someone she could love, someone who would love her. In New Orleans they drank *café au lait* outdoors and watched pigeons strut along the sidewalk. In San Antonio, drove among hills wondering where the city was. In his lunches sometimes he found her notes: I'll miss you.

But at the same time he realizes that something has shifted terminally in his mind, that despite these memories he is now looking ahead rather than behind. It is not what he wants, but it's what he has, what they all have.

A Brahms symphony comes on.

"Listen," he says. "When I was young, this was my favorite piece of music in the whole world," and he leans forward to turn up the volume.

"You'll disturb her," his wife says.

The lights of cars and passing billboards give to the drive their own pulsing, staccato rhythm, one in counterpoint to the Brahms he can barely hear.

"Have you ever been happy?" he asks after a while.

"Of course I have," she answers. "What a question."

Lights from an oncoming car blind him for a moment and instinctively he swerves to the right, then back. Soon they will be home.

Resurrection

Sheila killed a man today. Inadvertently, of course; nonetheless, there he is, dead in the pages of a major newspaper.

The call came at six A.M. Her editor gets up before dawn every day – opens his garage door to let the sun out, as she once put it – and cannot remember that others don't. Could she come in, he wanted to know, and write a retraction?

On a *Friday*? Sheila said. In the middle of the night?

The man's not dead, Miss Taylor. We've had calls from family, from friends, from his third-grade teacher. Finally he called, himself, to say that he was feeling much better now.

Give me an hour.

We need copy by eight.

She hung up and lay turned away from me, towards the window. Ice on the roof let go and sledded along it to crash onto the patio.

Problem? I asked.

Someone came back to life.

I thought at first, from her sadness, her distance, that she meant an old lover, but she turned and told me. How in a column she had mentioned this man, a painter once and briefly fashionable whom everyone, including the paper's arts editor and omniscient film critic, assured her was dead.

I didn't even write about him. You couldn't. There's not that much there, only what he might have been.

You're going to the office, then?

An hour. Less. Wait for me here?

As she showered and dressed, I stood in the kitchen grinding coffee, putting on water to boil, buttering toast. Outside, a squirrel threw itself between trees, and when it landed, falling in a slow arc through most of the visible sky, I found that I had been holding my breath. I thought of my own life.

Sheila was gone (sliding at that moment, though I didn't know it, over packed ice, a curb, a precipice) when I opened the front door to take out trash and discovered a man standing there.

No bell, he said. I knocked.

The front of the house stays shut off. Friends know to come around to the back. Others go away. Can I help you?

I was looking for Miss Taylor.

I'm afraid she's at the office.

Office, he said. Of course. As though I'd told him she was weekending on Mars.

I lowered the trashbags, supple and sleek as skin, but cold, to the step.

Can *I* help you?

He looked briefly at the bag, at my hands. You are?

Always a good question. I said: Jim.

He nodded. She writes about you.

Sometimes.

And I, he said, holding out a hand, am the late George Kelley. I am feeling ever so much better, he said. Neither of us laughed. He turned and sat on the top step, looking off into trees, a scatter of ice and snow on the ground beneath them.

I sat beside him. Copies of the Star-Telegram and New York Times lay in their white bags in the driveway. A dim pulse of music, Vivaldi or Telemann, came from deep within the house.

I read her column, he said. Have for years now. Never can figure quite how she pulls it off. You think she's going one way, then all of a sudden you're somewhere else. Memories and feelings you'd all but forgotten, ways of holding onto the world that you'd thought long since unraveled.

Perhaps you could give her a message for me, he added after a while. We sat together watching as a covey of blackbirds swept from tree to tree down the block. A truck piled high with brush and sod crept by.

Tell her thank you for mentioning me, he said. Will you tell her that for me?

I'll tell her.

And perhaps you'd give her this as well, he said, drawing a roll of canvas tied with strings like old maps from beneath his coat.

Well, he said, standing. I'll take those down for you on my way if you like.

We thanked one another and walked off with our small burdens, George Kelley down the hill and out of sight again around the street's slow curve, myself back into Sheila's house where, coiled in the answering machine, a call from the hospital waited.

Intimations

Sometimes the child, who has no name, bangs the tin can (for water) along the bars of its cage.

She has not been in the room, near the room, for months now.

Each morning before he goes to work he snaps on the leash and takes it for a walk. Raising a leg, it waters fireplugs, trees, automobile tires.

In some ways the child is very bright.

Though he tried, at first, they do not talk of the child anymore.

He feeds it at five each day in the little bowl with the Disney characters on it, table scraps and rich red meat. It hunkers in the corner of the cage, the far corner (to which it always carries the bowl), and shoves the food into its mouth with tiny hands. This lasts two minutes.

Its hands are dextrous.

Sometimes at night he goes in and talks to it. Business, that is what he knows, that is what he speaks of. The events of his day, the latest Dow-Jones, the new management position in the Midwest.

It lies on its side on the floor of the cage, looking out at him with wide, uncomprehending eyes.

But there is a spark of intelligence deep within them.

His own IQ has tested out at, variously, 121, 136, and

156; he does not know hers, but it must be high. (Often, he suspects she is more intelligent than he.) She has an M.F.A. They have built a studio onto the house. She spends most of her time there. It has a daybed.

He wonders at these times if the child knows who he is. Why he is there.

He suspects it does.

One night it reached out to him as he talked. Its hand struck the bars of the cage. It made sounds.

I – no longer can I accept the burden (I had thought it freedom) of an impersonal "he" – stand in the park at 12th Street and Forest Lane. While around me on this Monday morning range children retarding their journey to school and young girls (or so they seem) with bright cheeks pushing prams.

The air is clear and fresh, some freak of wind or other direction having borne away our accustomed weekend smog. Sunlight rests almost palpably on every surface.

And the child paces the leash. No longer does it pull against it, run to the end, or ferry side to side; this has not happened for some time now.

I stop, and the child stops.

Above our heads in a willow tree (I know this because the bronze plaque on the trunk names it) an adult bird – male? female? – injects half-digested worms (insects?) into the gaping beaks of fledglings. Far off to the right, a plane appears to be plummeting through the blaze of morning and into the river.

I whistle softly and the child turns from its study of the dragonfly buzzing its face. Eyes like spots of tarnish move to my own.

I walk forward and unsnap the leash, coiling it about my wrist. I suppose I wonder (I must) if I know what I am doing. Or why.

(The eyes descend momentarily, return to mine.)

And walk away from this.

Glancing back at the end of the walkstrip (yes, Lot; yes, Orpheus – see: even now I try to distance the real event with allusion, dead things) to find the child trailing behind me.

I lift my arms. Wave them wildly; stamp my feet on the pavement.

The child skitters away a few steps and ranges back.

And so – save me, that it should come to this; that I should have to confess it – I raised a foot upon which at that moment resided an Italian slipper of softest glove leather, and directed it towards the child's small, strange body. It struck him in the ribs; he fell.

Again and again I struck out at him and still he made no move. Six times. Until, on seven, his hand clawed at the grass beneath him. Eight, nine, he was to his knees, ten, his feet, running, eleven, going, gone.

Far horizons released the last captive strands of day.

And as he ran into them, I saw that he limped.

Into the room where I've never been, I move carefully. To see will these objects, forms accept me.

Light falls through orange glass and lays the head of a Renaissance lady dimly on the covers and green cushions of the daybed before me. In the corner beyond, stacks of newspapers and journals ascend, Babel-like, towards the ceiling. A huge ashtray supports a single smoldering cigarette.

On an easel by the window is a painting in progress. The background of park, grass, swings is well defined, the closer slide less so. On the slide a formless something courses towards the ground.

She is standing by the painting and, with but a brief glance at my face, passes beside me and into the hall. We do not speak. I follow.

Even before the door to his room, words do not pass between us, though perhaps at this point I nod once and quietly (I do not remember).

Silently she swings the door out, steps inside, shuts it.

Now she sits in the far corner of the cage, looking out at me.

I think there is a smile on her face and as her hand moves towards the tin can, I realize she is thirsty.

Need

He wasn't sure exactly when he had first noticed the child, but several miles outside Milford, glancing up at the rearview mirror, he saw her there in the backseat and realized that she had been there, an unremarked presence, for some time. Yet he is certain they had no child along when they checked into the Fountain Bay last night. He tries to remember pulling out of the parking lot this morning, looking in the mirror as he would always do. He thinks maybe she was there then. But he's still not sure.

The girl is reading a hardbound book with a green cover. There seem to be (in the mirror it's difficult to tell) dancing bears on the cover, a family of them perhaps.

"Good book?" he says after a while.

"It's okay, Dad."

"What's it about?"

"I told you yesterday. A daughter who vanishes without a trace."

"Do they find her?"

"I don't know. I haven't finished it yet, silly."

"I bet they do."

Beside him Rosemary's needles continue their minute orbits around one another. Whatever she is knitting now is green also.

"Always reading, that one," she says.

"You want to stop for breakfast yet?"

"Not unless you do."

"Well, let's go on another hour or so, then."

"Fine. We could stop at that truckstop just this side of Helena where we stopped last year."

"Sounds good. I'd forgotten about it."

Beneath bare trees the grass remains green. There are scattered small pools shallow as mirrors from last night's rain. From the radio come strains of a waltz.

Once, waking from nightmares of loneliness (he no longer knew how long it had been, or cared), he found Rosemary beside him, as though she had always been there.

They pass through a crossroads with a crumbling onetime gas station (tin softdrink signs still cling to its sides), Mac's Home Cooking 24 Hrs., a small wood church set up on pylons, a feed store. There is a mile or so of fence then, thick posts with single boards nailed obliquely between them, like mirror-image N's.

The girl puts her book down for a while and sleeps, curled into one corner of the seat. Rosemary pulls out an entire row and starts it again. He can hear the needles faintly clacking together.

They stop at a Union 76 for breakfast not too long after. The girl (Rosemary has started calling her Cynthia) does not want anything.

"Never eats anything, that one," Rosemary says.

There is not much traffic, and early in the afternoon a fleet of bright-colored balloons passes over. Behind them clouds gather as though towed into place by the balloons. At one point they follow a truck piled with sugarcane for several miles. Then they drive through a pounding rain back into sunlight. When they stop again to eat (and again Cynthia wants nothing) it is almost dark; the moon is like a round hole punched through the darkness.

They leave and drive into that darkness. There is more traffic now, as they near the city. He spins the dial between classical, country, jazz and rock, unable to decide. Billboards at the side of the road advertise topless bars, car dealers, restaurants and motels, Jesus, museums, snake farms. Cynthia wakes and asks, "Are we almost there, Dad?"

"Almost, honey," he says.

Beside him Rosemary winds in her yarn, tucks the needles away. "Try this on, Cyn," she says. He watches in the rearview mirror as his daughter pulls on the green sweater that fits her perfectly. For the first time he realizes that it is cold.

The traffic gets heavier. It comes from far away, tiny points of light like ideas. Then they come closer, and as they come, cars and trucks take shape around them.

Wolf

We had this arrangement. My wife lived six months of the year with her parents, the rest with me – I don't know why we didn't think of it earlier. The last I counted, she'd left me eighteen times. Another couple of times the folks came and (to use her word) removed her. They said I make her crazy, but *they* wanted to keep her a child. It's all really strange.

It was working out pretty well. I'm a freelance journalist, the kind others call a wolf, and in a bag by the door at all times I keep two suits, four shirts and ties, underwear, socks, toilet articles, notebook and pens; I can be on the trail of a story in minutes. But I could afford to turn down assignments when she was with me and double up when she wasn't. So we really had a lot more time together than most people do. It was great – movies every afternoon, hanging out by the pool when everybody else was at work, late-night strolls, breakfast at 3 a.m.

But slowly she began to hate me. I could see it deep inside her eyes as she lay across my chest in the mornings, a hard edge of self-interrogation. What would it be like without me; could she cope; how will she go about ridding herself of me – that sort of thing.

Then one day as we stood side by side in the kitchen preparing dinner (a corn soufflé, asparagus vinaigrette, pasta) she told me that she wasn't going back to her parents.

In a panic I tried calling her folks that night and got no answer. I tried again the next morning, that afternoon, and twice that night. Finally I phoned around and told everybody to get me some assignments, fast.

"Sounds like life or death," Harrison at the *Globe* said.

"For all I know, it may be."

"Even the best domestic arrangements can't last forever, friend, and you've been luckier than most."

I once knew a guy who had a big doormat that said GO AWAY. Nicest guy you'd want to meet, do anything for you, but he just didn't like unexpected guests. Suddenly that's the way it was with my editors. Delighted to hear from me, they'd chat along for an hour or more about things coming up, but for now all trees and cupboards stayed bare. I began to think horrible thoughts like city desk, food editor, *political analyst*. (Such was my despair and terror.)

It was about this time that I realized all the movies we were watching in those long summer afternoons were mysteries: a Hitchcock festival, Bogart films at the museum, Charlie Chan on TV. Books by Hammett and Chandler littered the apartment. Since bizarre crimes were a kind of specialty – I had a knack for somehow getting inside the criminal's mind and more or less writing from in there – in my leisure time, generally, I steered away from such preoccupation. But now I found myself scanning the dailies for just such accounts.

COWED HUSBAND SERVES POODLE
TO WIFE IN STEW

MAN TIED TO CHAIR AND *FED* TO DEATH

THE LAMP TOLD ME TO DO IT, MURDERER SAYS

That sort of thing.

Life between us, except for that knowledge like a drowned body deep within her eyes, except for almost imperceptible pauses before she replied (as though she were drifting towards worlds farther from the sun, and colder), continued much as before. In mid-July we attended a retrospective of horror films from the past forty years, in early August an "atrocity exhibition" (photographs from Auschwitz altered to show the prisoners with wide smiles and contemporary three-piece suits) at a local gallery.

In slow, plodding fashion I'd begun gaining weight from the food we spent hours in the kitchen preparing each day and from inactivity, from the sheer inertia of our days together. Talking it over, and reading two or three books on the subject, we took to running several times a day in the park nearby, circling again and again the park's patelike copse of trees and skirting narrow trails littered with family picnickers, scavenging dogs and benches carved deep with old lovers' initials. My wife quite early exhibited an altogether unsuspected natural gift for it, heaving out far ahead – a yard, two yards, steadily farther and farther – as I fell, huffing and lame, behind. Many nights she would go back out alone, saying that she loved to run in moonlight. At first, pro forma, she asked me to go along, but rather soon that civility (for it was no more) ceased; and this became, in fact, my only time apart from her, except in sleep.

Need I say that sleep was troubled? In one dream a man I knew, but whose face I could not place, stood on the other side of a locked door smearing the bloody entrails of a turtle against the glass, slowly robbing me of light. In another a child's legs were gone from the thighs down; only the bones protruded, and tennis shoes were laced to the knobby ankle sockets.

There was, too, the eventual revelation that I had not worked in almost eight months. Flurries of calls from editors had tapered off, then subsided, as I refused assignment after assignment; I could not now remember how long it had been since the phone rang. I didn't know, but thought that I must surely be almost out of money. I tried to recall what writing was like: bent over notebooks in cabs or planes or the bathrooms of hotels; the world that came into your head as you blindly strung together word after word and then, *in* those words, ever growing, appeared there before you, part of the *other* world now, at least as real as yourself. It was unimaginable. And yet for so many years this was what I did, what I *was*: a channel, a voice, a mirror at once giving back less, and more, than what entered it.

And if that was what I had been, what was I now?

Somber September slipped in through cracks beneath the door. My wife's time away from me, her moonlight runs, lengthened even as the days contracted. Our fare grew plainer, and we began foraging (though perhaps this is only another dream) in the gardens and basements of neighbors. Pounds fell away from her; she grew lean and brown. We seldom spoke anymore. I lay alone shivering against the night, watching my own breath rise in the air above me like a ghostly, insubstantial penis.

And now it is November, strangely my birthday. In the kitchen my wife prepares to eat. I can hear her but a wall away, padding about on bare feet (for she has given up shoes and, largely, clothing) as she makes that keening, unforgettable hunger sound. I hear her at the door, dropping (or do I imagine this?) onto all fours. I only hope that I can finish this, my last story, before the story ends. That is all I ask of life now.

53rd American Dream

Sunday and just like all the other Sundays: clouds hung in the sky like jowls or wattles, sky gobbled up air, its feet moved in the grass, it was going to rain. The children had already eaten by the time they got up.

In housecoat (brown check, Neiman Marcus) and slippers (gray plaid, Penneys) Mr. More walked into the living room (he looked like a Viking departing his ship) kicking aside the scattered bones as he came, noting on them the marks, the scrapings of teeth.

"Damn," he said at last, standing in the center of the room, shaking his great sleepy head. (He looked like a bulls-eye surrounded by the rings of furniture bones children.) "I wish you kids could understand how hard it is to get good help these days, then there wouldn't be any more of this. You're using them up at an awful rate, you know: do you realize this is the third time this month? Bedford Hills, Children, is running out of maids." And then because the speech was over, because it was nine in the morning, because he'd run out of words, because he looked like a Viking, he said it again, "Damn."

"We're awful sorry, Pop," Tom, the oldest, said. A trickle of blood ran down the hinge of his chin and splashed onto Tonto's palomino. Always a slow eater, littleJim was crouched under the coffee table, gnawing at a knuckle-bone. "But we were hungry, awful hungry. And we got tired of waiting for you and Mom to get up."

Mr. More rubbed thoughtfully, sleepily, at the Brillo-stubble of his cheek and chin; his hand came away scratched to a red rash. "Well, I suppose that's understandable," he said. "But get this awful mess cleaned up before your mother sees it."

An exemplary team (one envisioned now the yapping pursuit, the bringingdown, the snarling devouring) the children set to work, piling bones onto a red wagon, mopping at the blood with Scottowels. Tim, the youngest, leaned in a corner with the towels jammed onto his arms, going *click-click* each time one of the others pulled one off.

Mr. More turned around three times and went back into the bedroom. The book she had been reading last night was lying open on the bed (stories Jewish and Zen, yang and yin, fat and thin) with a broken back, but his wife was nowhere to be found. He walked around the room, opening drawers and doors looking for her, climbed up on a chair to look down into the light fixture (king-of-the-hill on a pile of bodies and pieces of body, a single live cyclops fly stared back at him and waved one of its eyelash legs frantically: *j'accuse, j'accuse*). Finally, catching a glimpse of taffeta foot from his maple perch, he realized she was sleeping under the pillow. He jumped flat-foot over the foot rail – shouting *Hai!* and *Hing!* – and came down in a crouch on the Beautyrest.

He reached down and lifted the pillow. "The children ate the maid," he said, and dropped the pillow back.

Minutes later it suddenly lurched and fell onto the floor. His wife stretched slowly and turned over (slowly). "Poor Griselda..." she said to the suspended ceiling with all its tiny sound-absorbent holes.

"No, Dear. They ate Griselda last week. This was Olga."

"Poor Olga..." She pulled the covers up over her and he could hear her sobbing down in her dark warm cavern. He dived headfirst onto the pillow, got up and went to the closet, which perforce *yawned* open. (A thin slice of darkness being closed on, now, by irregular white boxes ranked on the shelf above, the line of clothes anchored with clothespins to the adjustable bar below.) He thrust his hand, quickly, in and – quickly – out: jaws of clothespins snapped, a hanger fell rattling out of the bundle in his hand. (The closet was now in need of a new lower-left bicuspid.) His hand braved the depths of a box and emerged with a pearl-white shirt. He began dressing, diagonally, from the imported clockwork left sock to the hand-stitched right cuff and the tortoise-shell elephant.

He was standing at the mirror, filing down his teeth, when Tim came and stood in the doorway behind him. Tim was dressed in balls of bread which he had glued all over his body after slicing off the crusts. He looked like a renegade dandelion.

"Okay, Pop, it's all cleaned up," he said. "We saved some for you, though – it's in the fridge."

"Right…look, I'm not too hungry. Why don't you kids have it later? You can make a sandwich or something." (Page 119: "Parents must sacrifice for their children.")

Tim looked dubious. "We got catsup?"

"Sure thing."

He tilted his head. "Pickles?"

"Big sweet ones." (Page 143: "Often the child is reluctant to accept this sacrifice; a careful air of nonchalance on the parent's part is the most satisfactory, and the most effective, response at these times.")

"It's a deal!" and he shot away, out into the living room to tell the others, leaving a trail of breadcrumbs to find his way back.

In the mirror Mr. More saw his wife bound out of Her bed (36x72: the covers flapped like brown bats), race across the cold Montina squares like a cowardly Queen, and dive like perhaps Ty Cobb beneath His (40x80: the floor was 3-D, no goggles required, sparkly pearls in yellow phlegm). "Kamikaze cantcatchme!" she yelled in transit. Then, sweetly, from under the bed: "You remember when the kids brought that puppy home last week…?"

He opened a drawer and replaced his toothpick-file in the case among the rest, just below the rat's tail and just above the camel-hair navel-lint brush, slipping it into its loop like a toe into Indian sandals. (His pride was the two-foot-long emery board he'd bought off an elephant manicurist when the circus was in town.)

"Sure do," he said. "And a sweet, soft little thing it was, too."

"Yes, it was, wasn't it?" Her hand crawled out from under the bed, crept across the linoleum – then went scuttling back sideways, back under the bed, leaving behind something that looked like a misanthropic butterfly: her rainbow bra. The games were beginning, the Sunday games. The games. "But they wouldn't eat a thing afterward, remember? They're just going to have to start eating regularly, Bruce." She always pronounced his name to rhyme with *cruise*. "Three meals a day, no snacks, get their vitamins, get their iron. Can't let them wreck their health." Again the hand came creeping out only to dash back to safety. But it left behind, this time, two sharp rubber cones with plastic warts on the ends. The warts, Mr. More thought, were like hard pink raisins. Or like, perhaps, Bing cherries impaled on the ends of ice-cream cones.

"I think you're right," he said to his wife. "I'll talk to them about it this evening." He opened the velvet-lined jade-and-ivory case which squatted with springy S legs on top of the dresser, as though it were about to hop off. He took out his Sunday eyes and put them on. They were made to resemble the eyes of a potato ("The potato is an innocent fruit") and were gold, 23 carats fine (the 24th part being constituted of tiny silver stars). They stuck out from his face like mutant, misshapen corkscrews. He turned his face from side to side, admiring himself in the mirror. "Yes-sir," he said, "first thing this evening." (Page 654: "The casual ease of early evening is the most propitious time for family conference, and the dinner table perhaps affords the most comfortable and accessible opportunity.")

This time the hand *rushed out* (nails clattering on the floor) and *crept back* (dragging its thumb). A *tempo* was being established. Smack in the center of one of the Montina squares now, floating in the phlegm, were two mounds of collapsing flesh. Two dimples with Scripto erasers inside, Mr. More thought. Or demitasse saucers with little prunes on them inside the darker cup-ring. Or a plastic dog dish. A pale smear of blood tracked back toward the bed, mixing already with the phlegm, thinning the fluid, which then overflowed into the room, bearing chunks of pearl that whirled and spun like leaves, clicking against the doors pipes bureau bed shoes.

"And they'll listen, too," Mr. More said. "Or no more TV." (Page 4: "The simplest punishment is often the most effective.")

He removed hair eyebrows ears and put on his skullcap (*ibid.*). Then he stood staring into the mirror for several seconds. Finally, he reached up and removed his nose, moving it to the tip of his chin. Much better. *Much* better. A *timbre* to match the *tempo*.

Again the hand: the dash, the creeping retreat. So bold, so coy, so like a Restoration lady. Lace pants this time: a small pile of cobwebs on the floor. As he watched they dampened, dissolved, joined the blood and phlegm, strings of stuff like seaweed. The floor was yellow going orange, of a starchy consistency. That is to say, *sticky*.

"I think that's enough, don't you, Dear?" Mr. More said. "Shouldn't you stop now?" He walked back to the mirror and, one by one, unsheathed his teeth. They clicked, one by one, into the porcelain sink, almost invisible. White. White.

"Are you ready then, Darling?" his wife said. And then the surrender, the sweet surrender, ahhh, as one by one her legs came sliding across the floor and bumped with soft thuds (like huge spaghettis) into the waterpipes, splashing the orange blood-phlegm up onto the base of the walls to water the orchids blooming there. Sucking sounds. A toe fell off, and the toenail off that. Mr. More picked the nail up and put it in his pocket; it would make a good pick when, later, he played his harp, plucking the strings one by one.

He kicked the legs aside.

"Yes, Darling, I'm ready," he said.

"Then call the children." (Page 456, right before the good parts: "Whenever and wherever possible, satisfy the children's curiosity as to what goes on behind closed, adult doors; at all costs, avoid deepening this curiosity, this wanting-to-belong.")

Mr. More called the children and together they hauled her body up onto the bed – it was covered with cobwebs – and he beat her with the olive branches and peeled willow wands he kept in the cupboard while the children watched and applauded. She screamed magnificently this time; her body oozed phlegm and later gave out great clouds of dust that looked like brown feathers.

Later he played the harp with his teeth and the children applauded again. And after that, with toothpicks and red wax off Gouda cheese, they put her back together again. However. That is to say, all but one hand and a toenail. Mr. More kept the toenail and had a ring made out of it. And they finally found the hand when, late that night, it crawled into bed with one of the children (Tom, the oldest).

That night at dinner (veal in catsup and chowder in powdered milk) he gave them all a stern talking-to (*op. cit.*). And the next day, Monday (which was, incidentally, Columbus Day), he hired a new maid. She had white white teeth and flat nails, her hips were like a saddle, her nipples like chianti corks.

Genevieve was her name and the children loved her.

The Western Campaign

Plans continue on schedule. Today I defecated in the executive urinals, then excused myself from the office early, pleading illness, in time to pour whalebone oil into the VPs' crankcases. Their cars will go twenty, thirty miles, everything in order, before the engines fuse solid. Tomorrow I'll introduce ground bamboo into the cafeteria executive coffee urns.

This morning Zed called me into his office. You've not been with us long, have you, D, he said, British accent pushing words against one another oddly and clipping corners from the edges of things. The wall behind him was glass; he nodded amidst blue sky. Fish the size of his head were painted on the glass. But your work has been, a word I use neither lightly nor often, exceptional. I feel you should know that rather soon Morgan's will have an executive position available. Not something you're at liberty to repeat, of course. But I do suspect you're the man to fill that post.

This could mean the ruin of all my plans. See them gang aft aglay, again. I'll have to take care, draw attention away from myself, cut a few false steps. It's all a dance. I spent the afternoon arranging rendezvous with several of the firm's secretaries on Zed's behalf, at the uptown bar where I knew he was to meet his wife after work.

J's waiting for me at the apartment on Charleston, wearing white jeans and a T-shirt the color of morning sky, seated on the low cement wall. Flowers tremble in the breeze behind her. Bushes intricately intertwined with honeysuckle. As I come up the walk, she stands.

"I hope you don't mind. "

Shake your head no and step back at the door to let her enter.

Transition's been imperfect. Fragments remain of a previous life. This has never happened before. Should not have happened at all. Then why has it.

Just inside, she stops. Nothing familiar. The slate's been wiped clean, it's a different world in here.

She turns. I think how much I lose, going through these doors.

"You look good. . . . " She lifts her hand palm up, propping the sentence open. Like a door.

"Demetrius," I say.

She nods. "Demetrius. " On her voice I hear in that name whole lifetimes of foreign ships easing into harbor, men who've left behind land and its stable ways, women abandoned. I hear dark bars along a hundred waterfronts.

"It suits you somehow. "

She says this, then tosses white hair over one shoulder and leans forward, wrapping arms about herself. The arms are long and deeply tanned, with slender straight fingers. She looks like a Greek statue someone has bronzed. Once so pale and white that new sheets looked dingy, grey, beneath her.

You remember those fingers lost in studio clay. From them (fingers, clay) issued bowls, pots, mugs and cups at once misshapen and of a strangely pure form. Containers all, all of them useful. New things in the world.

She steps close and takes my hand. Late sunlight lies on this brown rug like a discarded newspaper. Minutes drop off the edge of the world. Stand there watching.

I think how people say "there's history between us," and how history is never what happens. History is backwards invention, envelopes where, serving as your own travel agent, you tuck away airline tickets, hotel reservations, discount coupons and car rentals (and, always, your own invoice as agent) for your trip to Now.

"Once I loved a man named Marek. "

"Yes," I say. "You did. "

"He has a new life now. One with no place for me. I'd be a non sequiter, an anachronism. Like Senators wearing wristwatches in gladiator movies. "

Glancing towards the window outside which, predictably (some things do still hold), another day goes down in flames, she takes my hand in hers and places them together on her stomach. She's become, herself, a kind of envelope.

After a moment I pull away my hand and go to the dresser. There under shirts fresh in paper bands from the laundry, burrowed in like field mice beneath underclothes and socks, are bundles of new bills. Fifties, hundreds. I scoop them out and give them to her. See her then to the door.

All this closed oak facing me down.

When parents died and money came to me I had no idea what to do with it. I'd been at poverty's door all my life. All I could think to do was turn it back on itself. I began chipping away at capitalist America.

Here's what happens then.

From the window Demetrius watches J climb into a cab in the street below. The cab is brown and white, owner's name stenciled on the fender but unreadable from up there. The cab's hire light goes off, it pulls into traffic. Two Gray Line tour buses fall in behind.

Demetrius closes the blinds. Demetrius who after tonight will not exist. Who even now begins to fade away.

Traffic sounds in darkness break and surge over him, like the sound of the sea far away, like all those other lives.

Now turn on the radio. Where friendly voices wait.

Career Moves

I advertised for a job as king and got one. It was a shabby little land, the flag one color, no motels for tourists, national library in a back room of the bus station. They'd had few applications, they told me. They wondered if it was because of their paltry crown, or if word had got out about the food. I told them no, I didn't think that was it, people just weren't changing jobs like they used to, things being what they were. They decided I was a great ruler and asked what was my pleasure. I've always wanted a boat, I said. They started in building a navy.

The ad said very clearly: Wanted. One Jim Sallis. To Start Immediately. Experience Required. Apply in Person. This is what I'd been waiting for. I tried calling, faxed, finally went on down there. The building faced east, and the windows on that side squinted against the sun. There were forty or fifty people inside, all with résumés and leather shoes. You want to take the test? a woman behind the desk asked when I got to the front of the line. I didn't know. Did I? Don't worry, honey, she said. No one passes it.

New trends in packaged products sounded like the way to go. They were a little vague about just what these products were that we'd be packaging, so I was a little vague in turn about my background and qualifications. This was only fair: I assumed we were negotiating. After a while they nodded to one another across the long table and told me they'd been looking for someone like me. I made it a done deal. We'd have to settle on a title of course. But I could go ahead and buy new shoes and polish the mailbox, take someone out to dinner.

Name three of my personal heroes. What was the last book I read. Where do I see myself five years from now. Complete this statement: I would give up everything for. I'm prepared. Have my pen, my No. 2 pencil, my list of phone numbers and contact people from past employment, references. I complete the application and begin answering the 48 questions on their personality profile. After a while I get up and go to the front of the room to ask for more paper. When I look up next it's dark.

I've wormed my way through all the interviews to the final one but now this guy won't ask me anything. He sits rocking back and forth in his high-back chair, staring across the desk at me. We thought we might turn it around a little, he says, come at it from a different angle. That's how we like to approach things around here. So why don't *you* interview *me*? See if the company's someone you want to hire on. I didn't have a chair that would go back and forth but I did the best I could. That was about the toughest interview I ever had, he said when we were finished. How did I do? I'll let you know, I told him.

Each morning I would sit in Carl's diner with my coffee and newspaper reading every ad carefully, circling those of greatest interest. I would make lists of jobs according to location or bus routes, lists of numbers to call and in what order, lists of what I needed to remember about each job. In the afternoon I'd call for appointments, or to inquire regarding previous applications. A friend used to insist, I suddenly remembered, that the best way to learn about a city was to study its want ads. If that was so, I must be an expert by now, I figured. There a print shop nearby? I asked Carl. I had some cards printed up down the street and announced a series of lectures.

Notes

1   It can hardly escape the reader's notice that the first and concluding words of the story are *nothing*, the former in a peripheral character's dialog ("'Nothing wrong with that'"), the latter in the text of the story itself ("That night by the moon's pale light he dreamed of nothing at all, nothing").

2   Here we encounter one of the first variants: "this" or "his"? The source text reprinted here is from Anvil & Stirrup, a small-circulation quarterly; between that and our best fair copy, an early draft on yellow "second" paper from the author's files, a number of variants exist, perhaps resulting from editorial changes, possibly from subsequent authorial revision.

3   The author had at this point just met Roz (Rosyln Robyns), the woman who was to become his companion for the rest of his life.

4   From his story "Wasp Pounding Stone Onto Tunnel With Tool": "Their life together was a landscape, Barbizon by way of Wyatt. From on high you'd look down on something very

much like Appalachia: hills unfolding into sudden groves, long-forgotten pools of still water, these soundless footfalls of history."

5   *Shirt.* Variant: an *r* appears in the A&S text that does not exist on the second sheets. Author's correction or editorial addition?

6   "Miracles happen in the corners of lives," the author was fond of quoting in these days. (Conversation with Eric Stall.)

7   "Waiting for the Echo" begins: "Tuesday night, early morning actually, 4:15, darkness rolling over to show its dull silver underbelly, Jan dreams that he is a corpse."

8   In his copy of John Banville's *The Newton Letter* the author underscored this passage concerning "tradesmen, the sellers and the makers of things": "They would seem to have something to tell me; not of their trades, nor even of how they conduct their lives; nothing, I believe, in words. They are, if you will understand it, themselves the things they might tell."

9   The author's phonetic spelling here prepares for the outrageous pun – *Dja startchur own shurts* ("Do you starch your own shirts?") is heard as "Did you start your own church?" – that precipitates a page of truly strange dialog and provides the story's plot.

10 "Destined as we are by fate and our own disabilities to be wrong, we might at least contrive to be wildly, brashly, definitively wrong. That's the full measure of grace given us." *Life: A Fair Copy*

11 *Civilization, elegance, and terror* – to invoke once again the encomium employed by University of Nebraska Press on its first slim volume of the author's stories and carried down, such that it has become with title and author's name a kind of single parcel, from edition to edition.

12 At this point in the draft a single oblique line scores across the following paragraph: "Perhaps our lives consist not so much of what happens in them as of the explanations and connections we make." In the margin is penned: "The same is true of deletions."

Octobers

He watches her walk towards him. There is a long, low hill and she comes down it smiling. It does not occur to him to go and meet her. Her hair is pulled back in a bun, as she said it would be, and she wears steel-rimmed glasses tinted light blue, silver hoop earrings, sandals. "Leona," he says.

(They will walk for hours among manorlike old homes on Swiss Avenue. Runners roll by them, darting and mutable as their own conversation. Over some lawns float pale globes of light. Then with no memory of transition they find themselves abreast a span of cheap apartments and sway-backed bungalows and start back.)

They stop at a cafeteria to eat. She speaks of her time in Cuba, Peru and India. Can capitalist society survive, can it change itself from within. He has assumed for many years that America is merely stilting over ruins. She has advanced degrees yet pursues no career, working instead in temporary positions because she wants no stake in this society.

They speak of Eastern philosophy, Merton, Max Picard, Thoreau. Of one another's childhoods, families, marriages, fears. He talks, as he did so often in those days, of Marx, never suspecting how soon what he spoke would leap from his books, from his thoughts. There are islands of terrorism during the Republican

Convention that year, riots in a few inner cities, university protest marches: American business as usual.

(She will walk among civilian patrols and endless fires, remembering his ready laugh, his sad brown eyes. She produces her papers on request and tells where she is going, where she lives, where employed. Says that yes, she knows she should not be on the streets after curfew.)

They walk past her house and she tells him of others who live there. It is fine, she says, except for cockroaches. The others, all women, are much older than she. They are teachers, secretaries, receptionists. The house is a modest, declining version of those on Swiss Avenue. Seven people live here, each with her own small room, her own unaccomplished biography.

(At two he will wake her to say the cell's been infiltrated, four of them taken, the rest in flight. He won't be around for a while, he tells her. The following morning, taken to the police station and questioned by a man in casual military dress, she knows nothing.)

Buses throw themselves past, dragging cars in their wake. There are no runners here, only occasional beerdrinkers on front porches or carhoods. There is so much to say; they want to know everything about one another. The moon crawls in and out of clouds like an insect bumping its way over driveway gravel.

(At last she will admit he is not going to return. She walks near his apartment each day, hoping to find old friends with some word of him, even rumor, but she sees only strangers. She awaits the sporadic postmen. He can't write, of course. But there might be a page of Thoreau, a quote from Hesse in neat calligraphy, an Eliot poem.)

Hours later they stop for coffee at an all-night café. Her fingers slim as she lifts the cup. And parting, she offers her hand; days later he recalls the exact warmth and pressure of it. There is no answer at the phone number she gives him. He waits. Days go by: soldiers, kites. She calls. She tells him she is involved with someone already, that she can't see him anymore. He says he understands. There is a long pause. She says, Today's a good day for a change.

(It will be over quickly at first, then more slowly as one by one in ensuing months, islands of resistance are overcome. Party leaders find themselves looking out at shattered buildings with amazement, faced with a rapid shift from rhetoric to real action: to governing this country *bouleversé.*)

The first day they're together twelve hours and the following afternoon together another way on soiled sheets in his basement apartment beneath a map of Russia in Cyrillic, tiers of books on brick-and-board shelves, a bust of Wagner with one ear missing. At first she talks softly, then falls silent. Her eyes close and, just as her body arches upward, spring open again as though something has leapt from them into his own. A jolt runs along his spine into his hips and forward, outward, closing the circuit. "Leona," he says.

(Years later, dying in another strange and torn land, he will say again, "Leona." He remembers for a moment how her eyes sprang open that day. His own eyes close.)

Afterwards they make tea and she sits crosslegged on his mattress cradling the cup with its broken handle in both hands. She's unwound her hair and pulled it forward over her shoulders; it flows into, joins, the other, darker hair at the base of her belly. Cezannelike, she has become a series of interlocking triangles: pubis, body and splayed knees, cupped hands and elbows – even her face clipped to such angularity by fading light. The world is geometry, he thinks. The world, he says, is geometry, weather, and misunderstanding: a few solid shapes repeating themselves over and over in the grey fog of a thousand formless things and thoughts, light forever fading.

(The revolution will last, will endure, three years. Then like an overturned beetle, legs flailing, the old society rights itself and goes about its business. Party leaders are taken into Washington bureaucracies, deposited behind computer-cluttered desks with secretaries who soon grow weary of filing nails and forms and, with little else to do, begin pursuing their bosses. Committee reports roll off computers on daisywheels and race over telephone lines to congressmen and "interested parties." The only true revolution is absorption, this purest form of dialectic.)

He has another forceful memory of her, one he'll extract again and again in that strange, torn land that leans down over his death. Waking, he finds himself alone in bed. She is at the window; he watches her long hair and half-turned face against the orange glow. There are fires everywhere, she says. Everything is burning. The past is almost gone, I think. She turns fully to him, a tear pulling at one cheek, one eye. What else do we have, Mark, what else but the past? Unseen fires turn the tear into a small sun there below her blue glasses, beside the silver earring.

(She will come each day to the beach. Only here can she be alone, without history, weightless. For the past consoles; it is history that bears things away. Behind her, fires still leap and churn against the sky. Fire details rarely respond anymore. The beach around her is littered with decomposing bodies of birds, fish, young people. She watches the sea hurl itself endlessly onto that beach and feels new life falling into place about her somehow despite it all, all these new lives taking shape now, breaking on the broken beaches of the old, endlessly.)

Enclave

A bright yellow room. The room is empty save for a table and two chairs, a bed, a small animal cage beside it, books. The bed is steel-framed, the headboard and base composed of slender steel rods; it creaks with every movement in the room, whether or not the bed is itself occupied. The cage is of the same steel rods, but painted a chrome-bright green (those of the bed are white), and is approximately 2 by 3 feet. It appears to be empty; but harsh, metallic sounds (gratings, clicks) issue from within it throughout the play. The cage is supported, at the level of the bed, atop a stack of oversize books like those which contain reproductions of paintings, or like "coffee-table" books. The stage is in fact literally overwhelmed by the *presence* and the *fact* of books; filled with them; they are piled on the floor, the bed, against the walls. They are of every possible size, yet each is either scarlet or sky-blue. Some are neatly, squarely stacked; others are leaning in disorder against the walls and bed; some are in precisely swirled columns, like spiral staircases, and reach as high as 8 to 10 feet. In one corner there is a pile of them, hundreds of books, paperbacks, magazines, dumped there at random and looking as though the entire mass would collapse were one to touch it, even come too close.

A woman is standing at the blank, yellow wall stage-right, dressed in formal eveningwear, staring *out*, as though a window existed there. A man is on the bed. He is naked, books piled under and around him. (Because of the books we cannot actually see that he is naked.) After several moments, during which the tableau is held, the man speaks. Even then, there is no movement.

– Well?

The woman continues to stare *out*. Finally he speaks again.

– What colour uniforms?

She parts her lips. Begins slowly, quietly.

– Pink...? No. No, they're naked. They're naked this time.

– Students.

– No...No, they look too young.

– Soldiers then.

– Some of them have painted the top of their bodies brown...

– Or veterans.

– Some of the children are wearing armbands...

– The old woman, is she still out there?

– She's making a speech. She has to stop every few seconds to put her teeth back in. They keep falling out.

Pause. The woman continues to stare fixedly at the wall. The man picks up a book, thumbs through it, tosses it back onto the bed.

– The bombs?

– Of course. You can't hear them? They haven't stopped for weeks now. Not for a moment, a second.

The man shrugs. Books shift on the bed, slide down his body.

– You get used to them I suppose. Don't notice. After a while.

– Do you think it's really America?

– Don't be silly. Who else would it be.

As he speaks these lines the man is pushing books away from him, struggling out of the bed. Several books fall on to the floor – the greatest quantity at the exact moment his *feet* touch the floor. Simultaneously the rest, those remaining on the bed, collapse together into a compost heap. The man rises and walks distractedly among the stacks of books, vaguely towards the tea table. (He contrives to remain partially under cover of the books, so that we never in fact see that he is naked at any time during the play.) The woman is still standing at the wall, motionless, "looking out."

– There's a priest...

The man begins to make tea. Sounds: the metallic clicks and grating from the animal cage (almost metronomic), the creaking of the bed at every movement he makes, the whistle of the teakettle. Absolute silence "outside."

– He's walking among the bodies. He has a ring on each hand. One has a question mark on it, the other has an x. Sharp edges, like razors. He's branding the wounded and dead. Whenever anyone argues with him he immediately pushes the x into their forehead. Or their cheeks.

The man is pouring tea at the table. The table and chairs, the cups are steel, the same colour as the cage.

– The farmers are standing around the rice paddies. They're throwing firecrackers when the others come too close…

– Ready dear.

– There's a sniper on top of the Eiffel Tower…

– Come dear.

– Indians are coming down the canals in canoes. They have crossbows. And beards. And steel helmets with horns on them…

The woman turns suddenly, goes to the table, sits. *Long pause.* The man and the woman drink their tea. *Long pause.* The sounds from cage and bed continue; also, the teakettle is still whistling. (It continues to whistle for the duration of the play.) Spoons clink, mouths slurp, the woman speaks.

– Where are the children dear? Have you seen them lately? There are ten…no, eleven…of them.

– What? I think they went out. To play. Are there really that many now?

– What? I think so. Yes, at least eleven. When did they leave?

– What? I don't know. A few days ago I think.

Pause.

– *You* haven't been going out. To work I mean.

The woman pauses, stares across the table at the man.

– What was it you used to do?

– I was a physicist.

– But what did you *do?*

Long pause. The man frowns in concentration; then smiles.

– Oh, you know. Entropy, information theory, stuff like that…I think.

The woman sips tea, stares into the cup.

– We're out of tea again.

– Mmmm. They dumped it all in the harbor.

– Sassafras.

– Mmmm. It's growing in the closet.

– Which one?

– Well, all of them as a matter of fact.

– The roach spray didn't work.

(He stares into his teacup.)

There is a crash, as of glass shattering, and a heavy object strikes the floor. The man leaps to his feet. The woman drops her cup, speaks.

– Mind the glass. It shattered the window, you might get a nasty cut.

– I'm not going near it. It might be a bomb.

– Don't be silly, it's a brick. Not a bomb. And there's a message wrapped around it.

– It could still be a bomb.

– But it's not even ticking or anything, it's perfectly quiet.

– So much the worse. *I* regard that as highly suspicious.

– It's a brick.

– But it has words on it. You have to admit it has words on it.

– Of course. A message would have words, wouldn't it.

The man pauses, considering:

– Not necessarily…What language?

– English.

– *See!* I told you. I'm-not-going-near-it.

They sit to their tea again. The brick remains on the floor, its message and presence ignored. The teakettle continues to whistle; the cage to give forth its clicks and rasps; the bed to creak at every movement the man makes. The woman begins to read from a newspaper. The man glances at the wall from time to time, nervously. They carry on with their afternoon tea. Finally the woman speaks, without looking up from the paper.

– Why don't you go look out dear. You look upset, that would help you.

– No. No I was…just…wondering.

There is a long pause; to the other sounds is added, now, the rustling of paper. After a while the woman says, idly,

— Someone just applied to Lloyd's to insure the human race.

— Incredible!

— Hmmm.

— They're still putting out the papers.

— Hmmm.

— We don't even subscribe to one you know.

— What?

— Where did you get it?

— What.

— The paper, where did you get it?

— O. It was on the floor, by the front door. Someone had shoved it under the door, I suppose.

— When?

Pause.

— I don't know. I just noticed it today, this morning, it could have been longer.

The woman pages through the paper:

— There's no date on it, anywhere.

— Of course not. There wouldn't be, would there. How would they know.

The man suddenly gets up and walks to the wall. As he "looks out," the sounds stop. The bed (which went into a frenzy when he stood); the teakettle. *Then* the sounds from the cage — he notices and turns very quickly. Walks toward the cage. Stands staring down at it.

— It died. You flushed it down the lav. Last week. Or the week before...

The man stares at the woman for several seconds, then goes back to the wall. Motionless there, he assumes the position the woman held at the play's beginning. Now we can hear the sounds outside. Bombs, shouts, guns.

A single scream.

Insect Men of Boston

Like a man at breakfast who looks up at his wife, Darling why is there a razorblade in my orange juice?

That wife on the living room floor with The Times spread out all around her. I just heard Beethoven's Pastoral Symphony on the radio he says, coming into the room, I cried.

"Penn Central is bankrupt."

"Why are they doing this to me?"

Communication then has again proved impossible o well. I shall go for a ride on the bus he thinks into Roxbury. And wear a white sheet. Do we have any other kind. Will my body to the university hospital and if she wants me she'll have to go through seven years of medical school. I'll deny that I'm married to her. Say I don't know this woman. I think I've seen her in my building. I think I've seen her with a child. It was probably stolen. Why can't they just leave me alone.

He has a ham sandwich for lunch. There is no bread and he uses a bagel. She comes into the kitchen for coffee. She is on a diet and has been eating toothpaste again. You're disgusting she says. "Yes would you like to go to bed with me." And that was the last cup in the set. O well. He goes to the window and pushes her plants out.

She is taking a bath. Yesterday, driving back from Concord, they saw a Madonna standing up in a tub among trees. The whole thing was painted blue. Would you like me to read you something? "Hand me my comb the big one." He looks down at the pile of clothes she took off. No there's nothing he wants to wear.

She is doing a new painting. But the subject she's chosen, a huge bottle with ferns, is too large for the canvas. And she paints on the walls. One fern touches a window: she takes the brush away, to step back and look. He raises the window. She paints on the screen.

When she moves the canvas, ferns and leaves remain behind on the wall and screen. A friend has accepted the canvas (which has become a Madonna with child) as cancellation of a debt. The friend frequently brings people over now to "see the whole painting" or "experience the totality." She is generally working, since it is the weekend and this is her only free time, and he makes coffee for the friend and his companions (remember that this is *her* friend, not his, he hardly knows the man) while they sit with crossed legs discussing the relevance and impact of this temporal disruption. The tension generated in the suspension of time between seeing the canvas and this, the rest of the painting. A valid, and heretofore insufficiently explored concept. One says. The friend manages this skillfully, often contriving to let them pass hours in aesthetic discussion before escorting them into her "studio" to reveal the rest of the painting. She has added apples and grapes to the limbs of the fern. References to Ovid are inevitable. So is running out of coffee. And the "fern" is becoming a mad horizontal tree. The friend has to move her aside to show his companions the rest of the painting. He is increasingly embarrassed, uncertain how much of the tree he may now fairly consider "his."

Why don't you ever write about me?

I write about your paintings don't I?

You can't write about paintings.

Of course I can. You're standing there. We've been married for six years. Your jeans are spattered with paint. It seems to be mostly green. Your hair is tied back out of your face. You're on a diet. You have two brushes in your hand, one wound in the last three fingers, I guess it's for detail, one between your finger and thumb. That's the one you're using now. You're not wearing shoes and you have on one of my T-shirts. Your breasts are hurting. You keep touching the left one with your hand. There are brown fingerprints all around it.

She drops the towel and begins flushing the toilet wildly, again and again.

What is your name? she asks. He shrugs and tries to cry, but he's forgotten how. They do The Times crossword together.

They go swimming. She looks like a turtle lying on the beach in the sun. Children are diving off the dam.

He meets her at the trolley stop and carries thirty pounds of mushrooms she bought at the Haymarket up the hill. She cuts off the stems and glues mushrooms all over the ceiling and walls of the bathroom.

What does this mean? he says. Holding a piece of bacon on a fork over the pan. Nude.

She stacks plums in the medicine cabinet. She puts her blonde wig on a cauliflower. She stuffs the toilet full of spring onions and closes the lid. She fills the bathtub with small pieces of cardboard that say "Frog." The other rooms with popcorn.

Last night they went to a movie. It was a very bad movie called Mainspring. An inhabitant of which kept saying Why are you trying to kill me I've seen you in the other room waiting to kill me. As that inhabitant changed its diaper his child talked about thermodynamics. And in the dark he put his arm around her, touched her breast with his fingers.

I will put itching powder in her bra. I'll go out at night and make obscene phonecalls to her. I'll put blood on the toilet seat.

She picked up his wallet and threw it out the open bedroom window. "Frisbeeeeeee."

When she finally came back he ignored her. She stood in doorways but he outwaited her. She took off her clothes and danced for him. She passed out on the floor in front of him. She put rubber bands around her breasts. She got a carrot from the kitchen and lay down on the couch, throwing one leg over the back. Hello he said.

What a sad thing, that tear in her pants. Where I could put a hand in her sleep now. Never know how kind I was.

She punches the paint out of the holes in the screen with a pin.

It's Sunday.

As a man might say I've found relief here, a harbor.

"It was an accident," she said.

Doucement, S'il Vous Plaît

They're forwarding me on to Versailles now. At least I think it's Versailles. I watched the postman's lips as he readdressed me, concentrated on the stammering pressure of the pen as it darted across my face – the *a*'s and *e*'s, unaccountably, in small capitals, the rest properly in lower case – and tried to ignore, to block out, *faire taire*, the dragging accompaniment from the side of his hand. And I think the word he printed, with his felt-tip pen, was *Versailles*. I felt the four strokes of the *V* and *l*'s quite distinctly; they were rapid, hard. That I am being forwarded is certain, for I saw the stamp descending like a dark sky and was able to read quickly, and backwards through the smear of ink before it moved away, leaving my eyes blotched with black, the words *priére de faire*. And if the next were *renvoyer*, there would have been no need for the postman's pen, for the additional letters among which I was able to discern only (I think) the single word *Versailles*; a simple circling, an arrow, should have been sufficient to send me on my way back to 1, Petherton Court, Tiverton Road. It must have been, then, *suivre*. So at least, for another day, another few weeks, perhaps my abiding fear – that I bear no return address and will end among the dead letters – this fear is allayed.

I am dropped from a box into a hot canvas bag. The smell of paste and ink, of dry saliva and, somewhere deep inside us, perfume. Apparently, while sleeping I have gone astray and been returned – to travel to some scrawled new address, to be set aside for inspection and at last referred back – to the post office collection box. It was the shock of falling through the slot onto hard edges and sharp corners, no doubt, which awakened me. The other letters will have nothing to do with me; they sense difference. And their language is unfamiliar now. Something guttural, that might be German. My questions go unanswered. Deep in the canvas (the perfume?) I can hear a British accent, a soft weeping, but am unable to make out the words.

I wait in a cold hall, propped against the frosted mirror of an ancient oak wardrobe near the door, for a week before someone finally scribbles *Not at this address* in a cramped, small hand, afterwards retracing several of the letters and scoring beneath them, four heavy lines which feel at first like rips then like deep bruises, and drops me in the corner mailbox on his way somewhere. The mailbox is round. British.

Why do they move about so much? How are they able; where does she get the money? And is there the faintest remain of a familiar perfume in this box...

I am being forwarded again. I have no idea where.

It is Christmas, I think, and I am lost in the deluge of mail. Crushed with parcels, shuffled like a card but never dealt. High in my solitary forgotten pigeonhole now, I observe the functioning of our postal service. It never before occurred to me how astounding, what an efficient, essential instrument of society, this service is. Or the complex problems dealt with each day as little more, actually, than part of the routine. I watch with fascination. Perhaps this is the work I was meant for.

I was a writer. More and more, my attention centered about the mail: my correspondence, the possible arrival of checks or hopeful word from my agents, rejected manuscripts that must be sent back out at once, copies of my books or magazines containing some small piece of mine, perhaps a foreign translation of something I'd done long ago and almost forgotten, packets of books about which publishers hoped I would be inclined to say something complimentary, a note of praise from some editor of a non-paying quarterly. The post was delivered twice daily, nine in the morning and just after noon. I would sit on the steps in the hall with a cup of tea, or the worst times, days I was definitely expecting something, with a drink, waiting. My wife and I got into shameful screaming fights over this, and once I struck one of the children who raced out of the flat before me and grabbed the mail from the postman's hands. (I always waited, looking away, until he had deposited it in the box and left the building; then forced myself to walk slowly to it, whistling, and to every appearance completely uninterested. I believed that somehow this outward display of unconcern would influence what was there.) After we left the States and came to live in London, things became much worse; my expectations more desperate. And while my wife was conscientious about collecting it from the box, that having been done, mail lost all importance to her, as though for some reason she could not accept it as a real thing, part of the daily discourse of our lives. Forced to be away from the flat during the time of delivery, I would return to look hopelessly into the empty box, and then to spend untold minutes searching the flat – for she could never remember just what she had done with it. Often I would find an important letter leaning against a dirty cup among stacked lunch dishes, forgotten. Others would finally appear in my oldest son's wastebasket, the stamps having just been torn away for his collection. Generally, considerable portions of the message were torn away as well.

Faces bend down and leer at me where I lean in the boxes. Shade light from the small window with their hands so they can see my diagonal cutting through the stream of fluorescent light from behind. Breath frosts the glass. Finally I'm removed between two fingers, crushed with others in a gloved hand. The thumb of the glove is empty and flops against us.

Later a man stands over me. All the others have been opened. They are lying, torn and empty, at one side of this table, and he is turning me over and over again in one hand, mumbling to himself, a pink plastic letter opener in the other hand that I see periodically, rising jerkily toward me as though by its own will, then retreating again from sight. Minutes pass, and the next time the hand appears, the letter opener has been replaced by a pen; then a rapid scribbling. He puts me down, goes away. From beside me, among torn bodies, comes the scent of familiar perfume. It is fading.

It would seem that I am in Poland. Or perhaps Yugoslavia.

I always wanted to travel. Jane and I would lie for hours in bed with carlights sliding in sheets across the walls and ceiling and talk of all the places we should go – making plan after plan and abandoning each in turn, as some consideration of my work intervened. Departures were postponed time and again, applications for visas were canceled, passports expired. Jane collected a sizable library of travel guides, two cardboard boxes full of travel folders. She became well known in the lounges of airports, ticket agents, foreign consuls. Soon she read nothing else, thought of nothing else.

"How were the children today?"

"They were in Hawaii."

Other places.

They're forwarding me on to Rhodes now. Ailleurs. Gdziès. I have no idea where. And my sole, my only consolation, is that somewhere, at the end of all this, somewhere my wife and family wait to receive me. I imagine how they will discover me one morning on the floor by the door, beneath the mail slot – perhaps they will have heard the outside door, the brass lid swing shut as I'm pushed through, even the sound I make striking and sliding out onto tile or wood, a few inches – and how then they will prop me up lovingly on the table between them; between, perhaps, the cornflakes and Billy's strained fruit.

The First Few Kinds of Truth

Five men are watching my wife walk down Rosedale.

One with a belly, one with an eye, one with an arm. The other two with legs.

(Look, it's a great idea, dynamite! We're putting on the play, see, I mean everything just like it was before, the way we've been doing it, but all through it these stagehands are carrying on parts of a body, you know, a foot, then a leg, a spare arm or two and so on, and they're putting them all together in the background, right against the drop, and then by the time the play's over, dig this, they've built a man back there. Maybe they plug in the eyes on the last line. And this guy they've put together, *he's* the one who does the curtain call. It'll knock 'em out, man. Have 'em up on the goddamn chairs clapping and shouting. The critics'll go wild, man, we'll get reviews like you've never *seen*.)

Five men are watching

My wife

Is walking down Rosedale to shop for food and pick up

(For a moment, minutes, she becomes a part of those men. For a longer time, their attention defines her. Does she notice. Does she know.)

her mail.

J. Thank you for the check. Sadly, it did not make the wolves go away – they are still out there, rattling all their keys and trying to pick the lock – but at least the goddamned bird has stopped saying "Nevermore, Nevermore," over and over again. Now it just sits there and says, "Well, maybe. But I doubt it." If you can't send more money can you send a new razorblade. I can't afford to buy one and all mine are dull – I've read that it hurts, that way. Love. J.

Five men are watching my wife walk down Rosedale. Her hips, which are large, sway slightly from side to side. Her leg swings out, forward, in, in a tiny arc; then the other. They end in small, perfect feet. Like the top of her body, also small, with breasts you can cup in two bent fingers. Under that white shirt. The letter is tucked into the hip pocket of her jeans now.

This is a photograph

It was sent to me anonymously this morning

But upon closer inspection is not really a photograph. Or not a "real" photograph. If I can put those two words together? Someone has used light, and only a laser could provide such tight focus, to create this "photograph" on a blank plate, "drawing" on the photographic plate with the light, just as one applies pen to paper. The depiction is perfect. The representation almost flawless. The men are there, watching, solid. Only a slight blurring around my wife's body.

Why is it, she thinks (with the five men watching), that the period just *past* in your life is always that which seems, *now*, most satisfactory? You made yourself go away from it, and it from you; yet now it seems to contain all the best moments of your life, all the times you were happy – and against all good sense, knowledge, memory. It assumes the proportion of an ideal now and, while it happened, was hell, of a kind. Surely it's not just the immediacy of the experience; an accumulation of information which hasn't become truly "past" but is in the process of doing so, and you *feel* that process, the sorting and sifting, on some preconscious level. Or the psycho/somatic ability to retain knowledge of pain only in the abstract (fully processed information). Or even the simple disorientation of always beginning again. When the difficulties seem for weeks, months, overwhelming, and the mind flees the present, goes back in abreaction to a time when things were at least a bit more settled, ordered in some *implicit* way however powerful the upsets, the arguments, the problems.

No, she thinks with the five men watching, it's more than that; those are only parts; there's more to it. But I don't know what. With the five men watching she remembers each dislocation, each move – each new home or apartment, with or without her husband, like a set of steps, nine so far, with nothing at the top. How each time, each place, for months it seemed that the time and place *before* was the best. And then the desperate letters, the phone calls at three in the morning, the promises spoken, forgotten, never meant. Because neither could change that much. Until the new days at last resolved, as they always did, into the monotony and vague, petty dissatisfactions which are *now*, "the present." One is "happy" only, she decides, in retrospect. Recalls her husband once saying that his major talent as a writer lay in creating instant nostalgia. (But why does everything finally have to wind up as words.)

Five men are watching my wife walk down Rosedale. She notices one with a mouth. The mouth smiles, opens the rest of the way and says Hi. She thinks of last night, the theater and afterwards, how gentle he was; the book he gave her. It is late afternoon. Perhaps she should write her husband a letter tonight. She just read a story of his in a magazine. It was about her.

Five men. It rained during the night and worms have crawled out onto the sidewalk, are lying there dead. She looks down to avoid stepping on them. She is barefoot and has startling blue eyes, carefully highlighted with mascara and blue eyeshadow, and a fine line of green on the upper lid. The soles of her feet are hard and can never be fully clean. She has a momentary fantasy of a single enclosed room in absolutely *perfect* ecological balance; bugs, spiders, snails, mice, cats, birds, green plants. Lots of plants. She grows avocados. She has just written a syndicated newspaper column, illustrations and all, to tell *other* women how to grow avocados.

(The technique. We pitch camp on opposite sides of the marital river and in the best Roman tradition burn as many fires as possible, to try and show the other side we have more troops, more strength, than we actually do.)

She has stepped on one of the dead worms after all. With the five men watching she swings off the sidewalk and wipes her foot on the grass *(never forget the way that felt)*, thinking of the collage she's just finished. The top is a photo of a crocodile partially submerged in green water, a black line bisecting the whole and the animal's evil black eyes just barely showing above the water's surface. Below that, she has cut out the second paragraph of the response to her application for a teaching position in studio art and drawn a black border around it. "Since you mentioned your acquaintance with Professor Lynn Jones and are living in Dallas, I feel I should tell you the tragic news that he died December 2 here in New Orleans at his residence of suicide. We are all still quite shaken by the loss of a colleague we admired so much." Her only thought upon receiving the letter was, He's the first of us, our friends, to go the way I'm sure so many will. Now with the men watching she thinks again, The first of many.

She stands with her classic profile turned towards them just inside the window of a Winn-Dixie, waiting for the machine to deliver Top Value Stamps, her hair long again now. (It was short, shingled, in the photograph.) Pays the eight dollars thirteen cents. Picks up the bag of alligator pears, mushrooms, milk, ground meat and eggs.

Five men are watching my wife walk down Rosedale.

There is a worm in her belly, planted there last night.

There is a rose in her teeth.

She is crossing the street.

She is trying to sing.

It is five o'clock.

(Applause.)

Delta Flight 281

As I leave my apartment on the way to see you, I hear the sound of heavy artillery in the distance. Two short bursts, a barrage, then silence. Far away, an aura about the buildings on the farthest horizon of the city, I see the flames still burning. Where the day went down.

Madam: We regret to inform you that at 11:31 p.m. last Thursday, the 4th of February, while crossing St. Charles Avenue, your husband was struck in the head by a passing idea. As far as we can ascertain, this idea had flown out the window of a late-model Chevrolet just then turning into Fern Street. Death was instantaneous; we are certain that your husband experienced no pain whatsoever and passed peacefully and at peace from this world to a better; we trust this will be of some consolation. Meanwhile, please accept our most sincere sympathies. Bureau of Ideas, New Orleans, Louisiana (Orleans Parish).

Mid-flight, with only twelve blocks remaining, the stewardess announces there is no more crabmeat for the canapes. Citizens (first class cabin only) in uproar. Shouts and threats, a few knives, broken two-ounce bottles of bourbon, Scotch, gin. I calmly suggest that we draw lots: We will pass out pieces of paper, on one of them will be a black spot, whoever gets the black spot will be slaughtered to replenish the supplies. My suggestion meets with approval all around.

Looking down on rooftops as we descend, I have the vague notion to write a novel, something which has never before occurred to me. Halfway through my third canape the stewardess comes down the aisle with a gun in one hand, a phone in the other, and plugs the phone into the console beside me:

"Hey there, Hector my boy. How's it going? Just wanted to let you know we just sold out the second printing. Great book, Hector baby, great! We're looking forward to the next one up here at Halvah House, let me tell you that! Well, be seeing you then, my boy."

As the No Smoking light goes on, the stewardess returns with a sheaf of telegrams: the reviews of my second book, which my new publisher has wired me.

At the airport I push my way through the women, reporters, literary hangers-on, decline offers to teach and look for a cab. I finally find one, reasonably priced – a '68 Ford, $750 – on the second lot I try. Driving through roadblocks and toppling camera dollies, with flashing lights behind me in the mirror, I head straight for your apartment. Make a good deal for the cab with one of the guys hanging around the corner newsstand.

I climb the ladder to your apartment, breaking each rung behind me so they can't follow. Throw my clothes down to them as I ascend.

I knock on your door and quickly step aside. *C-C-C-Cow.* Four bullets smash through the wood, stuttering.

Don't shoot again.

It's me.

Potato Tree

"We've found the problem," Dr. Morgan told me.

After a moment I said, "Yes?"

"Basically," he said, "you're crazy as batshit."

He was right, of course, but at ninety dollars an hour I had expected more. I waited. That seemed to be it.

"I see. Well. Is there anything you can do?"

"Oh, yes, a number of things. There are several quite interesting drugs on the market. Years of psychiatry – that might be fun. Shock, megavitamin therapy, behavioral training. Probably a lot of others. I'd have to look it all up."

He swiveled his chair to watch a traffic helicopter swing by outside the window. From his new position he said, "Of course, none of them will help any. You're crazy as batshit and basically you're just going to have to live with it, accept it. Here, I wrote it down for you."

He swiveled back and handed me an index card upon which was printed in large block letters: C A B S. Below, in a painstaking tiny script, were an asterisk and the words "crazy as batshit."

"It shouldn't really be any great bother. I mean, you'll be able to keep on going to dentists, reading cereal boxes, having regular bowel movements, humming old songs – all the important stuff. Just a little bit of an interpretive dysfunction, that's all. You just won't ever know if things are as they seem to you; they could be *quite* different."

He wet a finger and wiped at a smudge on the desktop.

"I, for instance, could well be a wig-maker. A canoeist. We may at this moment be the sole attendants of a missile silo in Kansas. Do you play bridge?"

"No."

"Good. Hate that damned game."

He swiveled again to look out the window.

"Is there anything else you can tell me?" I said after a while. "Any advice, recommendations?"

"Only this," he said. "Go with it, ride it. Enjoy it." He turned back to me. "Most of us live in a much duller world than yours, you know." There was something very like envy in the poor man's voice.

"Thank you, Doctor," I said, rising from my chair and looking for the last time at his wall of diplomas. "You've been a great help."

"It's nothing." He removed his glasses, breathed against them, fumbled in pockets for a handkerchief. "Give me a call now and again to let me know how you're getting along." He looked back at the smudge through clean glasses.

"I'll do that."

I walked a few steps to the door. There was no knob, only a hand protruding from the wood which clasped my own in a handshake. I pulled against it, opening the door.

"Don't forget your diagnosis," the doctor said behind me. I turned. The index card dropped to the floor and scuttled towards me.

The world looked not at all different, unchanged by my illness as it had been by my former health, in short, uncaring. The first elevator was full – all of them wearing the doctor's face, perhaps patients of his – and I waited. Eventually I made it down to the plaza and sat on one of the benches under a potato tree. Some of the hospital patients were having a wheelchair race on the grounds, pursued by grim-faced, limping nurses.

"May I join you for just a moment?"

I looked up into a face of great and radiant beauty, though pale. She collapsed onto the bench beside me.

"Are you all right?"

"Fine. Just give me a moment, I'll be okay. Please."

I spent the moment looking at the oxblood gleam of her boots, at the tug and thrust of sweater, into the depths of her gray eyes. Never had I felt more alone; my loneliness entered me like a bullet.

"Well. I proved they were wrong, at least," she said.

"I'm sorry?"

"The doctors...Listen, forgive me. I don't want to inflict you with my troubles. You must have plenty of your own."

"Not really. I'm crazy, you see: nothing can touch me."

I took out the index card and showed it to her. A potato fell to the ground at our feet. The index card leapt onto it and began to feed.

"How wonderful, to have an *interesting* disease. All *I* have's cancer."

"What kind?"

"The worst kind, of course, but it's still pretty dull."

I put out my hand and she held it, just as the door had earlier. We sat together looking out over the grounds as a light snow began to fall. Beside us the potato tree thrust into the sky as though *it* were a hand intent on tearing out that white down, intent upon opening it. The patients had turned on their nurses and were chasing them about the grounds, laughing joyously as they crunched bones with the wheelchairs. Children sat watching.

"How long do you have?" I said finally.

"Not long. They said I wouldn't even get out of the building, it was so bad."

"*How* long?"

She looked at her watch.

"Ten minutes," she said, floating into my arms.

Among the Ruins of Poetry

In a village deep in the jungles of central Peru, and nowhere else, grows an orchid whose flesh is more manlike than most. And yet more miraculously, from their earliest days these flowers develop the ability to form human sounds. For a short time they converse among themselves or speak with villagers, mostly silly, insipid stuff, then begin composing the lengthy, complex epic poems to which each dedicates the remainder of its life. Everywhere one hears these orchids mumbling obliviously to themselves.

Some time back, and tacitly, they had adopted this routine: if at eleven she rose to fill the tub for a bath, he would stay the night; if she did not, he would not.

Tonight they are reading, he Proust, she Cervantes, as they share a bottle of burgundy. Precisely at eleven she stands and walks into the bathroom. He hears the water begin its fall and then she is in the doorway: But I don't *need* a bath. I've *had* a bath.

He understands, and leaves.

That summer a dead friend comes to see you. He lectures you on classic German literature as you bring him cup after cup of strong tea. I know them all, he says. You show him a few recent poems. He says: I would die for these.

He cuts himself shaving and tears off a corner of toilet paper to apply to one of the wider nicks beneath his nose where it becomes a hinge, a valve, flapping open and shut against his left nostril.

Someone says: I wish I had given up earlier. It would have been so much easier.

The refrigerator in his new flat has the sound of a sneeze when it comes on. Branches against the window creak and caw in the wind like birds.

You could never sleep in her bed. You spent many nights there after you'd made love, watching the pale plane of her back, the dapple of leaves on the wall, and listening to the tick and twitter of her birds.

Unable to sleep you would pad still naked about her house, her smell on you, about you, like an aura, as she tossed and threw pillows, covers, from the bed. You came upon copies of your books in a corner of the bookcase.

You could never sleep in her bed. You sat listening to the tick and twitter of her birds resolve into morning.

Recently the *News'* chief reporter has adopted, as "the only system adequate to the disruptions of our time," surrealism. This has caused some problems, admittedly, as in his feature of two days before, an interview with a railroad tie. Yet he writes so beautifully that no one complains. And this is considered by many to be an improvement over his prior Marxism.

In the café the couple's eyes do not meet. They speak of many things: right or wrong, how children have been brought up, the responsibilities of freedom, taxes, a music lesson, literature, Salieri. They devour croissants and drink down endless cups of coffee.

The water brought them stands unmolested.

You have been away a while, reading Proust, and, coming back to this world, you encounter significant changes, you say.

Several nouns have become verbs; there are new, unrecognizable words and equally impenetrable uses for old ones; whole pages seem to have been removed from the dictionaries.

Even the alphabet seems *not enough*, you say.

Last year he contracted to translate all G–'s future novels, believing revenues from these would buy time for the completion of his own small books. But time will not be bought. G– has become a dervish – four novels this calendar year! – and he has no time for work of his own.

Even reading the newspaper reminds you of her.

That summer, that last morning, there was wind as now. On the bed you held her small breast in your hand for a long while afterwards, staring up at the limitless white ceiling.

The Very Last Days of Boston

That requires an answer.
Something.

Mason Terrace, where we all came afterwards – après coup, he says. Where the leaves this fall are skeletons. Where everything seems to have happened before; in that past we can't admit. Where the wind sounds like gills ripping out of the flesh of fish, and it rains. Where this morning the charred bodies of all the women I've loved come floating down the stream outside our window. Where women's remains go thump-thunk in the heart banks as we pass. Etc.

And don't think I haven't seen you waiting in the next room to kill me.

With this turtle staring.

Its blunt head is pushed against one side of the glass cube that contains it, at the center of the room. Its nose flattened against the glass and it never moves. Each time I cross the direct line of its vision, it blinks; nothing more. The shell has been expertly cut away, something I never knew was possible, and hangs on the wall above a Mexican cane chair. At the party tomorrow night it will become an ashtray. You have painted a Madonna-like self-portrait inside it.

Your hair is long in the portrait.

1. A man was cut in half by a window. But not to worry: his wife contrived a system of straps and replaceable cellotape by which he is capable of functioning normally; only in such acts as seating himself and sex does he experience difficulty, and must he proceed with caution. But there's more. One night when he puts his dentures in the glass alongside the bed they dissolved, and the new morning he found a goldfish in the glass, which is of course in reality a jar. He carries it with him from bar to bar now that his wife's left him, and drinks only with the jar and the fish on the counter beside his beer, cigarettes, good intent; beside the hand that is open and holds so much memory.

One of them finds divorce papers in a drawer of the desk. 6. The said Plaintiff avers that in violation of his marriage vows and of the laws of this Commonwealth, the said Defendant did: Offer such indignities to the person of the Plaintiff as to render the condition of the Plaintiff intolerable and life burdensome. The part after the colon has been typed in. The date of marriage has been left blank; neither of them knows. Folded into the legal document is a scrap of brown notepaper on which her mother has detailed, step by step (and they are numbered), just what she is to ask the lawyers, just what she is to do. He corrects several minor inaccuracies and signs the papers. He puts them back into the drawer. One of them answers the phone and says that No, Jane is not home to a confused male voice which will not leave a message. One of them finds a letter to her on the letterhead of his publisher. The answer to this letter is filed away in the same envelope, never mailed or perhaps later revised. What I want to know is why did you feel it necessary to lie to me and tell me you weren't sleeping with anyone else, when I never required such a statement from you. I tried to call you last night and again at 6:30 this morning – needless to say, you weren't there. Living with him for six years has given me a very low tolerance for lies. Perhaps if you were first, things would be different – but that's how it is. And it ends: I need you more than 2 days out of 14. One of them is the husband.

2. He's an electrician. He keeps sticking his hand into appliances and so on and getting shocked, and he discovers that this stimulates him. (Background on flagging interest in wife, poor • relationship, affairs.) So he hooks himself and the woman up to batteries and a series of induction coils: they receive a steadily increasing flow of electrical power – which ends in a high-amperage shock at the exact moment each comes. Over the months he rigs more and more voltage into the circuits; they need more each time, to come at all. Months pass. One night when they come, and it's great, the lights go off outside. The window dark. They unhook the wires, tear off the taped electrodes, walk to the window, look out. They have just blacked-out New York City.

> "Another month just left
> Its umbrella in the hall

And I can't get used to your apartment. (Just *in* it, you say.) I've taken a room across the street, where I'm obliged also to take weak tea each afternoon with the landlady and to have cheap gauze curtains on my windows (as though they were wounded). At night I watch you return to your apartment with other men. The shapes in your window, against the shades."

3. Women.

Women in boots to their knees or slacks and sandals. Women in Neiman Marcus gowns, women who know how to say no, women with green eyes, with small feet, with stockings that have elastic at the top and no garters, women with narrow hands.

Women met in elevators, you hold the doors open for them, women who look like Edna Millay, like Virginia Woolf, women turning back to look while they wait at the corners for traffic, women in windows. Women with things inside them. Women bleeding, women eating, women standing in front of a Stella painting. Women with their hands on pianos, arms, something else.

Women watching you through the doors of a State Hospital.

Women waiting.

(4.) "Pandora tells Jordan about kudsu. Back home. Arkansas: a small town cupped up against the river by hills, and a problem of erosion. From Japan (this is just before the war) officials import a green vine, but forget to bring along the vine's natural enemy, a pale red beetle. The vine now covers the hills – a cushion of green several feet deep, leafy pads like the ears of small stuffed elephants – and climbs the radio towers, kills all flowers, chokes the trees. People must go out every week and chop it back away from their lawns."

"There are twenty people living in the apartment now. Pandora writes in the bathroom, as this is the only quiet place. She has a shelf above the sink where she keeps her books and notes; on the door facing the toilet is a sketch of her done by Jordan, the breasts amazingly detailed, showing the stretch marks and the single long hair that curls down around her left nipple. Sitting here with all the others moving about out in the other room, she fills exercise books with poems and letters, using every part of the page. These are all addressed to men she has known – farewells there was no time for. Occasionally there is a knock at the door and she must surrender, for a few moments, her room."

"Jordan had always thought crocuses were insects, small, unseen things that clicked away far off in the bushes and trees. Once, just before the end, Jordan tried to leave the city. He went out into the country where one night the streetlights failed to come on at dark. He ran back to his cabin, turned on all the lights and wrote Pandora a letter, in which he questioned the ideas that had brought him there. He looked up at the hills then and suddenly remembered what Pandora had told him about kudsu. Terrified, he fled back to the city – back to Pandora – arriving before his letter. When it came he threw it into the fire and sat for hours with the flames in his face, shaking with fear. Pandora never saw the letter. The next day, it began."

I wander through your flat, looking for pain, assurance. There are times we've been happy. The way your skin goes over your hips. A letter from you one day in rain. And waiting for me at the airport. When we met by mistake in town. But that was before all this. Before it was possible to have nothing outside your window. And I've given the windows away. Some will be interested in trying to rebuild, even now. Let them.

5. They are moving the city again. For the third time this year the men arrive in their trucks and brown trousers, smiling. They drive their vehicles wildly, like Dodgem cars, against the buildings. Walls, windows, doors fall into the backs of the trucks and the trucks begin to move away, out of the city, to take them somewhere else. The remains are washed away by torrential rains, which follow.

Till someday I'll be found in a small dirty room in the North End (which they've put back together). Their heads will be lined up on my bookshelf – all those men, necks crusted to the bare wood–and when they open the door–it won't have a lock and their approach will be silent – I'll look up and say, Jane. That you've come back.

And the water will be coming into Boston Harbor, carrying French ships.

(Something about fish.)

Where it never rains.

Women waiting.

Hope: An Outline

I haven't named any of you. I never shall. And they should know that, by now, but keep asking. With their mouths and bright tools outside the small circle of light, and this chair.

Can I help it if your answers come walking out of dark subways at night. Alone, in white coats.

"What do you want from me, no, what do you really want."

(Just to get up every morning with the same body beside me.)

That was one exchange.

Another:

This morning I found a cup of coffee three weeks old in the kitchen.

I want to go back to the doctor and say why did you give me dark eyes.

I want to return my left foot because the socks you gave me don't fit.

That — then letters addressed to postmen, knees of women that won't stay together. Some things I have to tell you because I'm sick of being loved and you'd better listen. (They won't understand.)

That you tore me out by the roots etc. and I pressed my lips against one kind of wound, a female organ.

That the body will not go out of itself. Like the mind; but try. It will go only into hers.

That planes are arriving from London so fast the men on the field who wave them in have got their arms tangled together into knots.

That I threw your luggage out of the window.

Remember walking up out of the subway at night, holding his hand, afraid to ask his name, and does he have one. And so on. 36 cigarettes a day, more, 3 nights & the desk clerk's nervous. A man torn to shreds by wind on the streetcorner one afternoon. Some souvenirs.

The second day, and I still won't talk. No, there was no one else involved. I was alone.

They are drinking tea now, crossing off the questions already asked, rewording the others to fit. The first one's 13-year-old daughter is pregnant, the second is worrying about athlete's foot. Brushing ash off the white socks he despises.

"What do you want from me, no, what do you really want."

No, there was no one with me. I was alone.

They are playing back the tape from our last session.

The first one is tall and sad; he dislikes doing this. He watches my face from outside the small circle of light – and, then, there are brief silences. He knows that soon now the second will kill him.

They are playing the tape. They have forgotten me. And the first one is watching the second closely.

Go on.

Tell a story. It doesn't matter which, because you know a lot of them; and those you don't know, you make up. Don't give the characters names, because they might not like the ones you choose, and they could have had so many other adventures anyhow. Don't be too specific about places because wherever you look we've been there before. Give the characters proper motivation and be suitably mysterious about your own. Put your name at the top of each page and enclose sufficient return postage.

With the change of season your Snomobile converts easily and quickly to a lawn mower. Simply disengage *hasps* 1-5 and remove the Cab. (See Diagram 1.) This unlocks Blade W, which may then be lifted from its cradle (see Diagram 2) and replaced by Blade S. Tighten *bolts* 1-8. (See Diagram 3.) Your mower may be adapted to particular lawn conditions either by tightening *lugs* 1 and 2 (see Diagram 4), or manually, with the internal Lift Selector. (See Diagrams 5 through 7.) With the Lift Selector at full *Open* (see Diagram 8), your mower will easily handle inclines of up to 110°.

A concentration camp. It might be 1999, it might be Poland, it is December. There are two men alive. A German. A Frenchman. The Frenchman is a member of the Resistance. From time to time he walks to the small window and looks out at the snow still falling, says to himself very quietly *Non!*, then returns to sit on the bunk. The bunk is a slab of steel welded to the steel wall. The snow has been falling for as long as he can recall. Then he gets up, walks to the door and shouts out into the hall: *Non!* echoes in the hollow chambers of the building. It has the sound of a blank going off in a revolver. The German is bringing his dinner. Kosher salami tonight, Grenouille. It's kosher salami every night. He looks at the food, two translucent slices like congealed, pale red grease on a single slide of bread, and says to himself quietly *non*. They refer to one another as Gérald and Grenouille. Possibly this is because they have forgotten their names. Gérald sets the tray on the bunk. It, too, is steel. The ragged sleeve of his uniform touches the solitary wool blanket.

    – You will eat your meal, Grenouille.

    – Non.

    – You must eat your meal, Grenouille, or you will die.

    – Non.

    – But you have no choice.

    – Non.

    – Please eat your meal, Grenouille.

    – Non.

Gérald picks up the tray and starts to leave. Grenouille will never eat; he is afraid Grenouille will die. He does not understand that Grenouille would die only if he *did* eat: that this is all that keeps him alive, this choice of saying Non.

– Gérald.

– Yes Grenouille.

– Where am I, just tell me where I am.

– Where you were before. We have not moved you, I have received no orders to move you. You are where you were before. You know that.

– Then....I've forgotten. I....don't remember.

There is a pause. Gérald stares sadly at the food.

– Please eat, Grenouille.

He waits for an answer, then moves again towards the door.

– "I am a man, Jupiter."

– What Grenouille.

– Nothing.

Today:

1. ~~Take books back to library check out Neruda 'Heights'~~
2. Call dr re bloodtype
3. ~~Letters~~
4. ~~Ms to BRevuew~~
5. ~~Have lamp repaired~~
6. ~~Shop food (mushrooms)~~
7. ~~Pick up tree at D's~~
8. ~~Call J~~
9. ~~Go over to Hyannis P and bail water out of the gdmn boat~~
10. ~~Tape, cigarettes~~
11. ~~Movie?~~

Tell her that yes you will stay away from other women and questionable situations. You will try, yes, to become a better person, but you can't be sure;   how much of this is after all a lie. Imply that it may all be. You will do anything of course, but does she really want you to, to stay with her. She knows very well what you need from her. Will she give it and can she, without damage to herself. And naturally you can't live without her, nothing makes sense that way but you don't have enough however massive love for both. Amazing. Can she, and tell you, decide what she wants, what she really wants. Then go to bed with her. If that doesn't work, go away.

I am working in my room. I've got up early and there's much to be done. Still, the sheets of paper are slowly making their way from the stack on the left of my desk to that on the right, near the lamp. From time to time the phone will ring. An editor will ask is that poem ready. The one… And no, I will say; there's this comma…Ah yes, commas. Troublesome things. There follows a brief discussion on the role of the comma in contemporary writing, and the advisability of my foregoing their use; the example of Apollinaire. Finally I hang up the phone and continue work. A few more sheets move from the stack on the left, into the space before me, go away to join those on the right. This time it is the doorbell which rings.

A stout small man with a red face stands there smiling at me. In his hands he holds a bundle of papers which, upon my admitting to my name, he begins to disassemble. What I thought a bundle is actually one large, stiff document. It hangs from his outstretched arms now, swinging in the wind like a bedsheet set out on the line to dry. It is a summons, the printing in script. Your postal expenses, he says. Your rent, the typewriter, the tape recorder… I pay him – I can't afford the loss of more time which this document promises – and together we search for the line upon which I am to inscribe my name, having already admitted to it. This accomplished, I return to the study. It is ten. The stout little man drives past outside my window in a metallic-blue MG. The phone sounds, unanswered. I hear the morning post drop through the slot onto the kitchen floor but do not go down to retrieve it. I resume my work. The sheets of paper are now sorted by color. There are four stacks: top copy, carbon, drafts, notes and commentary. White, yellow, blue, pink. The doorbell rings again.

I open the door to find a sheaf of papers beneath my nose. They issue from a small feminine hand attached, in turn, to a tall blonde in bellbottoms and tanktop. Moonlighting, she says. Overtime, trying to catch up. I know it's Saturday and I do hope I'm not disturbing you at your work but. Well, these bills, you see. They have to be paid. We have coffee together and with a pad of my yellow paper, the paper used for first drafts and carbons, we detail the items rendered on the bills. I make a token payment and sign an agreement. The rest will be paid within the fortnight. It is, after all, so easy to sign one's name. One has done it so many times; it requires no thought. We kiss and the blonde rides away on her Honda. I return to my study. The stacks of paper have grown in my absence.

The postman rings twice. It is a special delivery letter. Again I sign my name. I have accepted this letter, I am liable to its content. We gave you service when you needed it now we need money please see that we get it. This is scrawled in ballpoint on a formal bill dated three months ago. The bill, at the top, reads Plumbing and Heating. I have never heard of the firm listed there.

The next is a mild-mannered representative from the utility companies. He has had the kindness to come out on this Saturday morning (though it is now afternoon) to inform me that, unless the companies receive payment within the week, my telephone, electricity and water will be taken away from me. The water, I assume, carried away in ponderous, elephant-like trucks, the electricity lured into bell jars and trapped there. I offer to exchange the phone, which I am willing to do without (it is ringing even as I speak with him), for maintenance of the other services. I will even surrender my water, as there is a lake nearby. But the electricity. I own an IBM, surely he must understand, my source of income, etc. He laughs at these little jokes of mine and descends the stairs to his grey Lincoln. I go upstairs and rip out the telephone wires from the wall, then into the basement to shut off the water main. I am complying to their requests, I am adapting myself to the demands of my society, to its norms.

The left-hand stack, the unworked material, approaches the ceiling. There are other callers. I listen to their demands, their explanations, their requests, I comply, I will meet my obligations. Yes. I sign my name again and again until, at last, it begins to look strange to me, foreign and new. That signature racing across scored black lines. I pledge my arms, my heart to science. My body, upon death, to the local University Hospital (thereby meeting the bill for my child's birth). They tattoo the sole of my foot.

I am in my room working. They arrive between stanzas, lines, in the caesurae. Each time I go down to talk now, I carry with me papers from that increasing left-hand stack, which I burn in the garden as they talk.

Then for several hours I am alone. The telephone will not function, there are no callers, I have crushed the clockwork of the doorbell and pay no attention to repeated poundings at the doors downstairs. I work. And the stacks are exhausted. They go into various envelopes and files and one, the top copy, distributes itself among a number of envelopes which I will mail when I am able to secure money for postage.

It is six. I am eating dinner in the kitchen when I look up from the table and discover a man standing at the window looking in at me. I go to the door and dismantle the locks, which I have bought on credit, just this afternoon, at the hardware store.

It is seven. He stands silently at the door and watches me. He is holding only an old envelope. On the backside of the envelope he has scribbled numbers and words. Our records show…He has on his list every art exhibit to which I have been, every concert I've attended, the title and performers of every record I own, the genus and size of each tree in my lawn. Yes, I ask. Yes.

He is silent. And silently continues to stare into my eyes and judge, with one sideways glance, the shape and size of my ears. He stares back quietly at my eyes. The light is on his face now. Yes?

And I wait.

Hazards of Autobiography

1

I WAS SITTING QUIETLY in a small café off the Champs-Elysées. From time to time a cricket would chirrup pickup, pickup, pickup, and groups of people would walk by the café singing. I was out of cigarettes, patience and sorts. Michele in the dark of that very night had gone off to Switzerland with the owner of a German brewery. She informed me of this in a note written with lipstick on our bathroom mirror. My skis were also missing.

A young man at the next table watches a girl who has just come in and now is being greeted by several of the customers.

Who's she, he asks his companion.

They call her Crow Jane. Supposedly she has some rare blood disease. Written up in all the journals, they say.

Fame. He peers at the cocoon of smoke enshrouding his friend. What are you writing.

A poem.

Looks more like a letter.

No, it's a poem. I'll break up the lines later. When I have more time.

O.

It's content that matters. You know that. Voice. Style. Approach.

O.

You could say that everything we write is a letter, in a manner of speaking.

At another table:

See, I come back to the house at night and I try to read what he's written during the day. He leaves it behind there on the desk. And it's getting stranger all the time; almost impossible to follow. I think he may be forgetting English again.

What do you mean.

Well it happened once before. Last year. We had to start all over again. Wawa, tee-tee and so on. Christ he's thirty years old. And yesterday he wrote the immigration bureau, applying for an extension of my visa, don't you think that's strange.

Quite the contrary. Seems eminently reasonable to me.

But I'm French.

Yes. You do have a point there. Still one can't be too cautious. Sticklers for detail, these French.

I have to admit he did some of his best writing back then.

At another table a man just dropped a bottle of pills. They rattled like maracas as they struck the floor and rolled. The man is becoming a deep and rather lovely shade of blue, weakly waving his arm in the air to summon the waiter. His fingers filled with gold wedding bands.

But the waiter has stopped at a table closer to me. He shrugs his shoulders in my direction and says to the man and woman seated there, He's listening you know.

I picked up my book and left.

2

I HAD JUST RETURNED from adventures in London and New York, Bretagne and Lodz. My beard was long, corners of my moustache caught in corners of my mouth, my hair bore burrs and briars from Camden Town, Notting

Hall, Park Avenue and the lower East Side. These included one particularly fine example, like a perfect sphere of gold corral, or the ball of a mace, from Meshed.

Now the nose of the plane dips once, gently, and I touch (my hand on the window) the edge of America.

I wore embroidered silk. My left hand was adorned with rings, bracelets, the watch you gave me, the right bare save for a childhood scar that crosses my fingers diagonally through the knuckles, a healed knife wound. I hold my hand out before me and the blood fills my palm for hours.

Guilt expires, even as air congeals away from the mouths of the jets.

But I returned. To you. Offered my passport to the man at the lectern there. *For* you. He was reluctant; at last took it. It came apart like a newspaper in his hands. You're traveling alone?

Yes sir.

Have you visited Pennsylvania before?

Yes.

And New Jersey? You'll have to pass through there you see.

Yes. Yes I know.

How much money do you have on you sir? And I search silk pockets. Assorted quarters, dimes, pennies of two sizes, a Churchill crown, a florin, francs, zlotny (several of these), one of the new tenpence pieces. Geometrical coins, coins without centers, coins with empty crosses for centers, milled, unmilled. They collect on the counter before him. With the side of his hand he slides them into a scoop and from there into a kind of plastic ant farm. Numbers accumulate beneath a red needle. Telephones ring. Lights flicker and dim.

I receive a handful of suspicious-looking currency, invitations to contribute to charities or to subscribe at fantastic one-time-only rates to magazines and join various societies, tax forms, overdue bills. Home at last.

And the purpose of your visit sir?

When I fail to answer he says, I have to put something down you see.

Would it be possible for me to get back to you on that? I ask.

Because this is today who I am: the man who gets back, the man who returns.

No problem. Absolutely, he says. Take this along with you, fill it out at your convenience. Drop it in any mailbox.

He hands me an envelope. Good luck sir.

With?

He waves his hand towards the doors. America is out there. A wilderness.

We can't be much help after this, I'm afraid. You've been away a long time sir. Things have changed.

O.

And an escalator bears me lumpily towards the top floors.

You are there, above, behind the glass. With fishnet stockings and a dress of green sequins. I have nothing to declare. The remains of London, the beautiful white ruins of America. And now through escalators, electric doors, walkways, hallways and people we rush forward together, our mouths opening round like those of fish, and we try, we clutch and move our hands slowly in the suddenly stale air, to embrace.

Behind glass the others applaud.

3

THIS DAY
it's bright and with streamers. Big machines go over our heads. And bundles up ramps on backs. These men like barrels with beer on their breath. A Rolls at the end of the pier with bankers in grey. How long does it take them to get that look about them, they all have it. While clouds roll like seals at play. Sun and blue clouds, a solitary gull.

Some of them wonder who I might be. I watch as faces find mine, watch as thoughts flare behind eyes and eyes move on. Like myself: the man who moves on.

Four of them mount a makeshift platform, as for parades. Grand hurried speeches are made. Phrases are dropped like coins into slots of cameras and microphones. When the crowd parts, I'm there. I gave her that dress. Strange she should wear it now.

So, she says.

Wait for the cry of a tug to die off harbor. That man with a clipboard under his arm in clothes like mine nods. Knows who I am. Remembers.

So you're off again, I say.

I won't stop trying. I can't.

Even now that you're no longer a believer.

He believes.

Hold out the book and wait for her hand to find it. And her mouth to wonder if it's what it is.

You finished.

Yes. It's the only copy.

Light catches on the stone in her ring as she opens the book, runs her fingers over pages. As though she can soak up its substance by touch alone.

So much noise here, so many feet and faces. People climbing the ramps now smiling. Flashbulbs and banners. It was quiet the day we left, no blue clouds like these. So long ago.

I didn't think you would come. Thank you, she says. And is gone.

Up here there is wind and my coat and the aloneness of harbors. Questions from the press, who have got on to me, that I ignore. As she goes up the ramp with the others, turning at the last moment. Sun and blue clouds in her glasses. Sun and blue clouds.

4

THIS MORNING when it has light and four men at the top of the hill there. Stand with rain running off their hats. Then descend, the container between them, bumping their legs. While clouds rumble grey bellies and people below look up expectantly. New-dug hole filling with water.

I can hear him from in here. He has found something to say after all. After much shuffling and scuttling about in his books, I should think. While his wife so patiently waited. Thank you for his wife. His voice sounds far off and soft. And while I am certain he says good things, he just goes on and on, like the rain.

Finally I rap at the bottom of the lid. Fine wood. Thank you for this wood. He leans close. Yes?

Father could I have one last look.

He swings up the lid and I open my eyes. Rain runs over them.

Are there many here Father?

A few, he says. Not at all a bad turnout for so poor and rainy a day.

I smell the brandy on his breath.

Thank you Father.

Rain strikes and slides over my eyes but I cannot feel it. I close them now. My last sight the onyx ring on his index finger as he eases the lid shut. For a time as he resumes I try to concentrate on what he says.

And finally this.

Father.

Yes my son. He leans close.

That's very nice. Thank you.

Yes my son.

But can't we just get on with it.

Yes my son.

Another sound replaces his voice now, a sound just as soft and distant and welcome, a sound like the rain. And that's the dirt coming down.

European Experience

It's happened again, I'm in bed with a stranger. Don't know her name. If I want to remember the curve of the bottom of her breasts, the way they rest on her ribs or rise to her shoulder, I'll have to reach out and touch them. Do I know her? She has a name, an address (which she refuses to give me), three telephone numbers at which I might reach her. Along with the last she has given me a chart showing the time of day I'm most likely to find her at each number. She has long hair. She is wearing a tight violet dress. Her eyes are green.

Also: I am being pursued. I saw the frost of his breath on the glass just a moment ago. Her lover, husband, father, friend? How am I to know? Each time I try to confront him, he flees. Last week in the press of crowds at 14th Street he took the only way open to him and was crushed to death in the doors of one of the uptown trains. His last words were I kept my promise, Tell them. My suit is still stained with his blood. And for a moment I envied the dead man: he kept his promise, I must live up to mine. The next morning there was a certain wariness to his movements.

She has small breasts. When she lies down they hardly exist. Her hips are wide, thighs full, the whole lower half of her body out of proportion to the upper – breasts, slender torso, fragile arms. She is nude in the photograph, I can't remember what clothes she wore that day.

Someone has written a collection of short stories and published them under my name; they have even put my photograph on the back cover. I received a copy in the morning post. Anonymous, no return address, postmarked Grnd Cntrl Stn. The stories reveal the most intense and intimate movements of my life. My attorney is investigating the possibility of a lawsuit against the publisher but, as the work was copyrighted in my own name, there seems little we can do. The publisher expressed to my attorney his admiration for the book and desire to meet the author, relaying an invitation to a party at his home last night. Where I met this woman.

He follows me everywhere. Perhaps I am looking for associations where there are none. Perhaps he is nothing more than a hired assassin. Plotting my rotation around the events of the day. Then, certain, he will strike.

She was standing in a group and said You're here, You finally came, and took my arm. She was in the park by the lion-pawed fountain where we watched pigeons dive for pennies then silently walked away together. We were afraid of words, I think. It was a clear blue day, the water silver. It would never rain again. She was in the library. We had requested the same book and sat side by side at one of the long tables all alone in the vast Special Collections room. She was working at a restaurant, to show me the way to the table where we never arrived. She was beside me on the plane from London. She was sitting on the fire escape, crying softly, and I opened the window.

They are moving the city again and I am occasionally lost somewhere between her place and mine. It was at one of those times, coming up out of the subway into what I thought to be midtown Manhattan, and finding myself in the open space of Queens, that I first approached my pursuer. He turned and threw himself onto the back of a truck just then pulling away, carrying off the skating rink from Rockefeller Plaza.

Her hair seems a different length and color each time I see her. Her neck a perfect curve, wing of a sparrow. Her eyes are astonished. They move slowly, as though through room after room after room.

Ice crashes off the roof and onto the ground outside. There are pigeons frozen alive inside it. She is gone. He has taken the photograph. He has gone away himself. And I am sitting here saying _____. Her name. And it all makes sense.

It does, it does.

I am waiting for a train to take me a little farther away. Here at Paddington Station. Out of the taxi with my single bag. Ducking. Halfcrown tip, smile, Ta. Now I'm larger, on the pavement walking away from the cab. Before that was a coach from Brighton, whatever I was doing in Brighton, and an 82 bus. Now I'm smaller, inside the vaulted station. And I'd like a ticket please. Certainly your destination sir. Anywhere. Ailleurs. I see and would that be return fare sir. No. I see sir that there is a departure from Gate D at eight o five that would be just about now sir the train arrives I forget where he said or when if that would be satisfactory sir. My hand pushes money through the grate. Stamp rubber ink. Have a pleasant journey then sir. Enjoy. Now down through Gate D and onto a coach and into tea to look out at the backs of all these houses with gardens and gates and clotheslines wondering do I have my passport. Vowing to be more careful what I say.

I am French, born in a large wood house off the rue de Tournon in the 6th arrondissement, of a Polish mother who died, passing her frail substance on to me, as I came into being, and of a father who as he said belonged too much to France to remain there overlong. He read to me, peering over the slats of my petit berceau, Cendrars' "Prose du Transsibérien et de la petite Jeanne de France" and "Les Pâques à New York," and when I was 6 it was to New York that, bundled up, with my French abécédaires and my grammaires anglaises, I was sent pour faire de l'éducation. To that place that could never exist, that was something created only for Cendrars' poems, surely. That about to acquire a history, like myself, possessed already its ruins.

Do you still sit daily on the beach with your book and glass of green tea. That strange beach with rocks instead of sand. The people around you like rocks themselves, steaming faintly in the sun. Where I told you one day Your ears are like shells and you turned back to me in the sun and your copper sweater and smiled. Then looked in the water and it carried your face away. Do you still believe, you said it once, that I'm forever returning. And when you are lonely, when narrow room and beach overcome you, do you still go down to watch the London trains arrive.

I am English. Turning over my passport at the embassy. We trust you've given this matter serious consideration young man. Yes, yes I have. And your wish is to carry on. Yes. Well then. You should be receiving the new passport within the fortnight. Through the he pauses here other he pauses again embassy of course. Which should I suppose be requiring new photographs. Yes sir I'm off to that now the little shop just up the way on Oxford. That would be the one across from Heals. Yes sir. Splendid. Best of luck young man. Enjoy.

He won't be coming round anymore, you understand. You can put your favorite records back on the shelf with the rest. You can stop rolling new paper into the typewriter every day. You can put away the French grammars, the Polish dictionaries, that clochard of a thesaurus, even those wretched Cézanne reproductions. He hated them too.

I am in hospital in Poland dying. They have scraped out the inside of my chest like seeds from a melon till there's nothing more to scrape out but moi-même. Soon my heart will relocate to Berlin, my lungs learn Japanese, my eyes look out on Brazilian rainforests. Three times a day doctors gather at the foot of my bed and talk quietly among themselves. I lie here reading Bergson. Duration: the official biography. I know they are bargaining for the many pumps pedals and organs of my body. Wypusc mu flaki. I am 24. Led to slaughter, I almost survived.

Down stairs. Black cab waiting there in snow. Gray sky above.

I'm an American. Your passport sir. Thank you. Welcome to New York. Sky and buildings locked irrevocably together, profiles of a single face. No beach here. But against the pale sky, just over there, she weeps too, this lady who, like myself, came all the way from France, home.

The car died again today.

Each morning the grocer leaves a pound of coffee and a carton of cigarettes outside the door for me. Mail is delivered with the morning papers. Today none were there. And there is nothing on the radio.

Or perhaps, to be precise, it died last night. In the dark and cold and snow. In bright sun I gently pried apart its hood, cleaned the plugs and checked they sat firmly in place. Dried out the carburetor and blew into the fuel pump, opened the feed a bit wider. Scraped the battery terminals and choked it manually. It wouldn't come around.

Nothing on the phone but recorded messages. Then Let It Bleed, playing over and over.

K came. As always, punctually, at ten, with breakfast in a paper bag. The perfect curve of her bottom like an inverted heart. Sitting on the bed she tells me how much of herself she leaves behind in these rooms.

Why do you keep coming here, I ask her.

I say: A whale's penis even in repose is taller than I am.

But what else could I do?

She holds one hand in the air and, with it, the other; as though some element in this action – connection, superimposition, the reaching itself – explains everything.

D will be expecting me she says, looking at her watch, I must be off, I really must.

Later now. Darker. I have moved away from the window. K, nude, is painting them black. One breast is set lower on her chest than the other and a bit to the side, nearer her arm. The nipple of that one is inverted, the other 3/4 of an inch long. D, she tells me, has strong fingers.

They came for the car, dragging it away across fields of broken cornstalks through snow. It left a thin trail of oil behind.

Trying to start a fire, I drop the last match just as a snow-laden branch crashes to the ground outside and look up at her. Why do you keep coming back here. The radio begins to speak again of the weather, how it will change.

The pills. A white one, a green one, a red one. They are lined up as always on the bedside table. Light nudges at them, at the table they are on, and retreats to the room's corners.

She is wearing grey slacks tonight, of a thick material that follows the taper of her legs down to fit close about the ankle. Where there are white socks, tops turned down, and loafers. She is smoking. Her breasts move inside cashmere as she inhales.

Other times she would dress in black and prowl about the house in pitch darkness, changing the furniture inside rooms, and he couldn't see her. He would hear the sound of her breath in the dark, the rasp of wooden legs. Once, lying beside him in bed, she told him of her plan to have a peacock tail tattooed in full color on her bottom. Or she might just turn up sometime, and maybe she'd been gone for days, with her pubic hair shaved down till just initials remained. Maybe they would be his and maybe they wouldn't.

Artaud at his last reading in Paris. He'd been locked away in asylums for nine years, all the Paris elite came. And every few minutes he'd stop and look out at the audience, out at Gide and Breton and Jean Paulhan and Camus and Pichette and his friend Adamov and the others. And he would try to explain, When you come round you simply cannot find yourself again. Life itself has been permanently debased, and a portion of original goodness and joy lost forever. He would say, I have agreed once and for all to give in to my own inferiority. Then he would stop and look around at all the lined faces. Putting myself in your place I can see how completely uninteresting everything that I am saying must seem. What can I do to be completely sincere.

She is sitting up in bed as he tells her this. Smallness of her body in the tall window now, framed there as in a painting. Motel sign a smear of red on the glass. A single tear like a glacier courses down her face, which she turns away.

She would come back with her body bruised and torn. No explanation, I am doing what I must. What else could I do.

Living now in this old house in Pennsylvania. Peirce's house, of much the same vintage, just down the road. A plaque out front gives the official biography in four sentences. Peirce who himself put it in three: Actuality is something brute. There is no reason in it. I instance putting your shoulder against a door and trying to force it open against an unseen, silent, and unknown resistance.

So let me tell you how it will be. One night you will be lying alone in bed. You will hear sounds downstairs. You will hear feet coming slowly up the stairs. You will hear them pause at the door. You will hear the doorknob turning. You will hear the door open. You will hear the footsteps again, on the rug now. You will be lying alone in bed. You will never see his face. You will never know his name.

The Good in Men

From my desk I see the red flag shaking itself like a fist in the air above our new capitol. I fear, in all truth, that the revolution is badly off course. "Bloody Boris" has taken to powdered wigs and robes, Manuel lies about all day in a bathtub in the council chambers, Hans has become a kind of manifesto machine, fueling himself with tarry black coffee for the day's writing. And I, of course, have withdrawn to this attic, these memoirs.

Most of the reporters are gone now. After the takeover and a few human-interest pieces, there was little here for them. One, a young drunk named Billy, remains. The revolution's never over, he says, until *after* the reporters leave.

Food is again in the city: potatoes, cabbage, some carrots. In order to have my time wholly free I have made up a huge pot of soup (for the water must be boiled anyway) and simply warm it when hungry.

In truth I am seldom hungry, or aware of hunger at any rate, for the work absorbs me utterly. I have just detailed the second month of the revolutionary congress when Jorge (may he now rest) fought so hard and long for Article Seven, and in writing of it I found all the voices, the clamor and excitement, the *faith*, returning to me. I do not know where that faith has gone; I cannot recall its passing. But it is with me only when I write, and when I stop, blinking out into this bright day and working my fingers to get blood back into them, it fades quickly.

But I find that increasingly (as now) my pen wanders from the history to memories of days before the revolution began gathering, and of the year we spent together. Do you recall the screen we built and handpainted during long summer days, and how we set it up before the fire all that winter in the huge living room; how we pretended we were in some tiny pauper's room? 'Til finally the paint cracked from the heat and started flaking away.

You should not have fled, Monetta. You did not understand what momentum our beliefs had – that for the first time a revolution would occur unoccasioned by actual hunger or grave social discord, but by simple desires to set things right, to create a moral order.

The revolutionary's goal must be to create a world in which he is superfluous. We seem in many ways, surrounded as we are by good men and virtuous action (and with thought towards the idle posturing of Boris and Manuel, the self-contained dynamo that is Hans), to have succeeded. In other ways, I have no doubt, we have failed.

In the final hours of Jorge's marathon filibuster and fast, he had to lean against the podium and hold on to it to remain standing, for of course if he no longer stood, the floor passed to another. Sweat had long ago soaked his clothes and he gave off a rancid, sour smell. For many hours he had recited from memory great portions of *El Cid*, Euripides, Plato, Santayana, Rousseau and Voltaire. Then he took a long breath (there was a hush of anticipation throughout the hall) and said: "In short, my friends – we must love one another or die." General applause broke out in the assembly. "Brilliant," one of the councilmen was heard to say. "Auden," Jorge responded, and took his seat.

Mixed with my memory of the smell of the bread we baked together is your own smell, and the scent of honeysuckle on the wind that last night we walked in the garden of what is now the capitol. You had knocked at my door (for I was then greatly occupied with the coming change) to tell me you were leaving. I hope so much that you are safe, that you've found a place there in the old world.

Soon, I think, I must return to the capitol, to our old home. Once we give ourselves over to history, history from that moment claims us entire. One day they will sing of you in the streets. How could it be possible for men who have been so important, men who have changed the world, to resume ordinary life as ordinary men, *however* they might try? I have been told that several days ago Hans looked up from his desk in tears, saying: "But I can think of nothing else to write!" Manuel has quit his tub for the hockey field. Boris comes daily to my room. Enemies of the state are abroad, he says. We must turn them out; we must "dress them in scarlet."

Moments of
Personal Adventure

Propellorman does not want to marry Lucy.

But just now, plying his trade, he faces an expanse of dark glass and the light-studded world beyond.

"You have to understand," his host says, turning briefly to the window against which the city throws its bright self silently again and again. In soft light his hair gleams with health. His motions are graceful, almost athletic. "At age nineteen I had an idea, a single idea; it came to me as I rode the escalator to work one afternoon. Within three months that idea had become this company, myself its president and principal shareholder."

He holds his brandy up to the light. "You're certain you don't care for some?"

Propellorman shakes his head deferentially, smiles.

"The rest is largely silence, Mr. Porter. That single day, that one idea, has been my life. And the years since, only a waiting."

"For what, Mr. Mills?"

A smile as finely turned as French curves. "What do we *all* wait for, my friend? Salvation. An end to our pain and confusion, to our hungers. Some explanation for all this."

He places the snifter squarely on the blotter before him and leans, one inch, perhaps two, closer.

"I hope you'll not be too harsh with me in your article, Mr. Porter. I am not, generally, so melancholic an individual. My wife has just been admitted, for the sixth time in as many months, to a psychiatric hospital. I seem quite unable to help her in any real way, for all my resources. And should one be of an analytical turn of mind – a curse I indeed carry, though a quality of which my wife seems wholly innocent – then after a time one comes to reexamine values, to wonder if everything one has believed and lived might not in fact be false, fleeting, futile."

"I understand."

"Somehow I believe that you do. And I thank you once again for coming."

Propellorman leaves him there in that dark room and rides the elevator steadily down. It is brightly lit and smells of cigar smoke.

Near the entrance he comes across a bar and goes in. Eight or ten real wood tables, Doré prints on papered walls, Vivaldi. All his.

He never takes notes during an interview but afterwards scrambles for the nearest shelter to write down, as quickly as he can and often virtually verbatim, all that was said. It's a habit begun, like many others, in college, where he'd sit in the student union following American Positivism or Anthropology 402 and fill page after page of his notebooks (always, even then, yellow) with Peirce, Dewey, Australopithecus, Sapir-Whorf.

Sitting at the bar (the bartender doesn't even get off his stool behind it), he orders a beer and begins writing, two lines of precise script between each blue-ruled line. Orders a martini and writes more, some of it just as it will appear in the final piece, some only an associative word or phrase, ragends of description, brackets with nothing inside them.

Once he thought he might restore the world to readers with his language; now he knows that often he will only further obscure it. They will come to his words expecting him to say only what they already know, and even if he does not say it, that is nevertheless what they will hear, until finally the words will not bear even their own weight. But once, in an essay on living alone, he wrote one sentence of absolute truth, and it has haunted him since.

He is a man who has been much loved by women, and now, after many years of living apart from and alongside them, he loves two. Lucy is bright and childlike and cannot do enough for him, with him. In Valerie there is something fatally damaged, a wound deep at her center that sometimes surfaces in her eyes. With Lucy he knows the world is good; with Valerie he understands the tremendous, silent struggles that make it so.

Gradually he becomes aware of the woman sitting beside him, knows she has been there for some time.

"Welcome back," she says. "To the world."

"That obvious."

"Yes."

"Well." Propellorman looks around. There is danger everywhere, his archenemy a master of disguise. Nothing is what it seems. "Another drink?"

She nods, hair tumbling over the distal shoulder. "If you'll let me buy *you* one."

"Done."

Something, then, of Alphonse and Gaston, neither willing to accept the final drink till at last, mutually befuddled, they lose count of rounds and agree to call it even.

Her apartment is on the second floor above a florist's, a single rectangular room long enough that light coming in the windows at the far end tires halfway across the floor. Low screens, makeshift bookshelves and a scatter of bright rugs divide the room into ragged continents. Everything – walls, screens, shelves, floor – is painted white. There are no chairs. They sit on stacked mattresses by the windows drinking coffee, words rushing in to fill the space between them.

Poets console us, Apollinaire said, for the loose words that pile up on earth and unleash catastrophes. And so as the night deepens, they move closer, bailing words out onto the floor, hoping to stay afloat.

There is more coffee, then scrambled eggs, then a long-reserved bottle of wine.

"I have to tell you," she says beside him. "There was…an accident. Please."

He opens her shirt and follows the web of scars across her breasts (nipple torn from one) and down along her body onto her legs. In this lurid windowlight the scars seem to have a life, a luminous existence, of their own, and he finds himself responding as he had never known possible, with an urgency he could never have imagined, almost as though propelled by something outside himself, some terrible, irresistible force.

"Who did this to you?" he asks long afterwards through the darkness.

"I did," she tells him. And later: "Will I see you again?"

But he doesn't know, doesn't know anything now, and so he doesn't answer, letting the silence carry whatever message it will.

Later, back at his own apartment, he'll wake at three with a terrible thirst. For a long time he'll lie listening to feet on stairs outside, to the sweep of traffic. Finally then he'll rise and walk uptown to Horse's studio with its smell of sour wax and manifold mirrors. Horse, the sculptor, there among his ravaged steel bodies, will know what to say, will surely explain it all to him.

Marrow

Il fait beau, the sea is calm. Earlier, snow was falling, *dans la mer.* To vanish. The ocean taller in its coffin, rising. A few single notes, and the air sustains them—fall of snow falling, no girl for my arms. Gulls tiptoe along the railing. Want to be skua searching the Arctic, white across miles and miles of white tundra, human heads to defecate on. They are riding with the ship to America: immigrants with tiny passports tucked beneath their wings. After disgorging us the ship is scheduled to return the Statue of Liberty to France; and perhaps, disillusioned, disheartened and disappointed, a few of the gulls, a few friendly pigeons, will return as well. Now the holds are closed on thousands of copies of old *Encounters.* Ballast. And behind us, in London, the bear and deer are moving slowly inward towards the heart of the city.

I am talking to an Indian girl; her clothes stitched full of mirrors, returning a sense of separate selves. Each tiny mirror lightly tinted, each a different color. She is smoking a pastel-orange cigarette, the base of her fingers imbedded in a ruby, holes drilled through to form a ring. Smoke now, like a momentary veil among her fingers. My breath on the glass. Gray in the gray of mirrors, and the green of the sea. While round and round the deck rides a cripple, shouting military commands. His legs are missing from the knees down, and the pedals of his bicycle are fitted with clamps into which the tips of his crutches are inserted, then strapped. He has been cycling around the deck since I boarded at Southampton. It's a child's bicycle. Just the steady thrust and drag of his shoulders against the crutches, and the shouts. The chest of a wrestler. And my breath in the mirrors.

– And your father?

– Yes. Military adviser after he was captured by our troops. He was much respected.

– A prisoner of war.

– Yes…that, at least.

I break off conversation and a solitary gull falls quietly into the sea from the top of the mast; seconds later, a melancholy cry, as another plunges after it. The two white bodies float peacefully together on the surface of the water, gently moving away from one another in the wake of the ship. Her hip against the railings.

– I'll see you for dinner, I say. Though I won't. And I have never seen her in the dining hall. Perhaps she eats alone in her room; there is some religious, possibly a medical reason, for this; that I am intruding? On her privacy, her faith.

She smiles, and the pale cigarette goes over the railing. The ring moves slightly along her fingers towards the knuckles and settles back as she raises her hand, slides it once across the space between our eyes; a cutting edge of softness.

– I am afraid I must dine with my husband. To see then my confusion: she moves her hand towards the cyclist, who is just now coming into sight around the contoured corner of the deck. That curves, like the thickest part of a bird's wing.

– But he…

– Yes. He is like that. A man full of power. I realize now how loosely her gown fits her, that the ring at one time would not have moved on her fingers but fit them perfectly. I smile and start away as she lights another cigarette, this one ochre. And then in the hallway outside my room, to stop and read the letter. Again.

J,

I received your gift this morning. Something of a shock, but a welcome one. And lovely. I suppose this letter will finally find you in some country neither of us had ever heard of – if it finds you at all, if the postal services are indeed still functioning, as they say – and I hope you find what you need there, or have found it already.

I was never able to discover what it was – I realized that this morning, sitting in the early light, pressing your gift against my cheek – and for that I'm sorry. Perhaps, in time, *you* will be more fortunate. Probably.

It's gone terribly cold now. Clouds with horrible bloated bellies. All the small surrenders of a winter that's finally come, like guilt. I sit and listen to the grass that grows inside the walls. I found a shirt of yours today in one of the cupboards.

I won't ever blame you for leaving. I took too much, and what you most needed; I should have been a mirror and was a stream. But your face stays with me. And…

C'est la calme qui m'étonne. And here I am. And nostalgia, for the comfort of lies.

Something you once said, about the bones, "my little monument not quite complete."

Good-bye. I loved you. And you loved. And if only I'd listened. And understood. So that's what I am....

Il faut faire équilibre.

Yours.

The room is hot and dark, but empty. I take off my clothes and lie on the top bunk, staring up at a faultless steel ceiling. I think of the girl standing up there above me, waiting. What colour cigarette would she be smoking now? Violet. Like her eyes. Lanterns. She would have turned a little further towards the rail. And others – others would be talking to her now. And all the time that little man going round and round on his cycle. And gulls, dropping off the mast, one by one, alone and in pairs. I look for a moment at my white suit hanging strangely on the back of the door, so light that it moves gently, rippling, in the air that issues from the grill close to the floor beside it, below the dressing mirror.

I lift my arm and the stump extends an inch above the buttoned sleeve, as though severed by the light from the window. *La main coupée.* I raise the other and put it behind, to pretend the hand is still there. And move the fingers, light glinting in the rings which cover each one. *Je suis l'homme qui n'a plus de passé,* I say quietly. I am the man with no more past. And laugh, at what follows.

We're a hundred miles out from New Orleans, where the statue lies waiting. Through the porthole I see even now the first signs of land – birds, shaped clouds, a ship – and hear the boat just beginning to lug in the backwash. After a while I get down and open the cupboard by the mirror. Far off there is the sound of a foghorn, like the cry of one enormous gull. I take out the small metal case and slowly begin to assemble what it contains.)

James Sallis has published short stories, poems, translations, essays and other nonfiction in publications ranging from *Ellery Queen's Mystery Magazine* and the *New York Times* to *The Georgia Review*. His books include eleven novels, multiple collections of stories, a biography of Chester Himes, three books of musicology, and a translation of Raymond Queneau's novel *Saint Glinglin*. For several years he wrote a regular books column for the *Boston Globe*, and still reviews regularly for the *L.A. Times*, *Book World* and others, as well as contributing a quarterly review column to *The Magazine of Fantasy & Science Fiction*. Jim teaches at Phoenix College in Arizona and at Otis College in L.A. He also works as a musician, performing solo, as a sideman with various bluegrass groups and singer-songwriters, and as a founding member of Three-Legged Dog, a trio of multi-instrumentalists.